Girls Know How

Super Science Girls!

Written by
Ellen Langas

Ellen Langas

Cover Illustration by
April D'Angelo

A Kids Know How® Book

Kids Know How®

NouSoma Communications, Inc.

©2017 NouSoma Communications, Inc. Printed and bound in the United States of America. All rights reserved. No part of this book may be reproduced or transmitted in any form or by any means, electronic or mechanical, including photocopying, recording, or by an information storage and retrieval system – except by a reviewer who may quote brief passages in a review to be printed in a magazine, newspaper or on a website – without permission in writing from the publisher. For information, please contact NouSoma Communications, Inc., 500 Waldron Park Drive, Haverford, PA, 19041, 610-658-5889, ellen@nousoma.com.

First printing 2017

GIRLS KNOW HOW® and KIDS KNOW HOW® are registered trademarks of NouSoma Communications, Inc.

ISBN-13: 978-0-9743604-3-0
ISBN-10: 0-9743604-3-0

LCCN: 20169138425

ATTENTION SCHOOLS AND ORGANIZATIONS: Quantity discounts are available on bulk purchases of this book for educational or gift purchases. Special books or book excerpts also can be created to fit specific needs. For information, please contact NouSoma Communications, Inc., 500 Waldron Park Drive, Haverford, PA, 19041, 610-658-5889, ellen@nousoma.com.

Proud supporters of *Enactus*.

Contents

Dedication

To girls everywhere who explore, lead,
achieve, and make the world a better place.

With special thanks to Sylvia Todd and her family
for sharing her inspiring story.

Much appreciation to:
Sally Bovell, Stephanie Campbell, Veronica Campbell,
Dede Crough, April & Chris D'Angelo, Brian Fillion,
Matt Fillion, Rachel Hoffing, Eugenie Lucq,
Dr. Pat McDonnell, Treacy McDonnell,
Natalie Mortensen, Laura Munts, Rupal Patel,
Cole Reilly, Julia and Keira Sherwin,
Kristen Stewart, Rita Wilson, Patricia Woody

1

"Maybe you should measure it first," Kristen said, while trying to conceal her panic at what was about to happen. Her best friend, Sylvia, was kneeling on a kitchen stool, holding an open bottle of vinegar over a mini volcano. Earlier, they had created the volcano walls from a mixture of flour, salt, and oil. Then they filled it with water, red food dye, and baking soda. Now the mound was standing tall on top of the countertop in Sylvia's kitchen. A light cloud of flour still hung in the air.

"It's okay," Sylvia said, half listening. "People make food with this stuff. What could go wrong?"

Kristen considered this but had her doubts. The girls had found the experiment on the Internet, and if everything worked as planned, the ingredients would erupt and spill down the sides of their volcano.

The two had known each other for as long as they could remember. Their mothers had met at a neighborhood book club, and their families quickly became friends. Born just a month apart, Sylvia and Kristen had always been inseparable. Kristen had recently turned twelve, and Sylvia would do the same at the end of August, just three weeks away.

"I want to get some good video of this," Kristen said, as Sylvia carefully poured vinegar into the volcano, where it would create a chemical reaction with the baking soda mixture.

Sylvia agreed. "Good idea. This could be the perfect experiment for our science fair competition."

Kristen grabbed her phone and aimed it at the volcano as both girls braced themselves for the explosion.

They watched.

They waited.

"Nothing is happening." Kristen's spirits sank as she stared at the still image on the phone.

"Just wait! Something will." Sylvia glanced at the directions and then back at the volcano. Still nothing. She held the vinegar bottle high and gently tilted it.

"Whoops!" she exclaimed, as a stream of vinegar splashed into the volcano. The concoction began to bubble and a sudden burst of red "lava" exploded, causing the volcano's walls to crack and spill across the counter.

"Look out!" Sylvia cried. "Get out of the way!"

"I told you to measure it first!" Kristen yelled as she backed up, knocking over a stool. Sylvia tripped over it and fell into Kristen.

Untangling herself from her best friend, Sylvia asked, "Did you get the video?"

Kristen spotted her phone under the counter and rolled over to grab it. The girls watched the small screen intently as she hit play, only to see a shaky video of the wall, the stool, and the floor flash by.

"I needed a better camera," Kristen said. "Someday I'll have a real one, like they use on a movie set."

"I think you might need more than just a better camera!" Sylvia teased.

The two burst into laughter.

"Girls?" The pleasant voice of Sylvia's mother calling from the front door brought the giggles to an end. Sylvia's mother had gone shopping, and they hadn't expected her back so early.

"Yes, Mom?" Sylvia called out, smiling at Kristen, who started to laugh again. Sylvia reached over and covered Kristen's mouth, trying to help her friend stifle her laughter.

"What is going on in there?" her mom asked, as she dropped her handbag in the hallway outside the kitchen. Luckily she didn't walk any farther.

"Um, nothing," Sylvia said innocently. Kristen's expression was angelic, and she mouthed the word *nothing*.

"I'll be there in a minute," Sylvia's mom replied. "I just want to take the plants I bought out of the car and water them first."

"Okay, Mom. Good idea, take your time." The girls looked at each other with relief.

Sylvia jumped to her feet. "Quick! Grab towels and let's clean up this mess!"

Red slime was dripping off the counter and onto the floor. Sylvia hurried to the sink and grabbed a dishcloth, while Kristen scrambled into action and armed herself with a roll of paper towels. Together they made the volcano disaster disappear in minutes.

"Hi, girls." Sylvia's mom walked into the kitchen. Mrs. Petersen was dressed casually in a blue and white striped button-down shirt over a pair of dark blue jeans. Her brown wavy hair, cut just above her shoulders, was starting to show the first hints of gray, the only sign that she was nearing fifty. Her work as a high school English teacher enabled her to enjoy having summers free, and she spent much of her free time outside in her garden. She smiled at the girls as she removed her sunglasses and placed them on the counter along with a bag of groceries. Sylvia cringed as her mother surveyed the kitchen.

"Hi, Mom!" Sylvia replied with such unusual enthusiasm that Mrs. Petersen looked at her with a raised eyebrow, wondering what the girls were up to.

Kristen just smiled nervously.

"What's that on your shirt, Kristen?" Mrs. Petersen asked, pointing out a red stain the size of an apple.

"What, this?" Kristen looked at the red lava stain. She tried to keep her expression blank.

"That?" Sylvia asked, to give Kristen more time to think of an answer.

"Yes, that."

"Oh, this stain," Kristen said slowly, as she looked down at her shirt and considered how she should explain the stain without getting into trouble.

"Yes, girls. That stain."

"That stain would be from my pen, Mrs. Petersen," Kristen explained as she made up an excuse. "My red pen."

"Yes, the red pen," Sylvia confirmed. "It was an unfortunate accident." She bent her head in sympathy. "The pen leaked."

"Very unfortunate." Kristen nodded and bowed her head, too.

"A lot of ink for one pen," Mrs. Petersen said, as she pulled a bag of potatoes out of the pantry to begin making dinner.

"Yes, ma'am," Kristen said.

"And I see the red pen also got on Sylvia's shirt and a few dish towels," Mrs. Petersen noted. "I think it's probably time for Sylvia to help me set the table for dinner. Why don't you girls get Kristen cleaned up before she goes home?"

The girls couldn't get out of the kitchen fast enough. They giggled as Kristen washed up in the bathroom. Then they hurried to the front door.

"That was a close call!" Kristen whispered. "Do you think she knows?"

"Of course she knows, she always knows!" Sylvia whispered back.

"That was fun!"

"A blast. But I don't think we found our science fair experiment yet."

"That's for sure. I'll see you tomorrow!" Kristen said, as she walked out the front door.

"Good! What do you want to do?"

"We could look for an experiment," Kristen suggested. "I saw a perfect one that involves building a rocket ship."

"Cool, let's do it!"

"See you, then!"

Mrs. Petersen finished peeling potatoes and opened the trash can to throw away the skins. The remains of the volcano and red-soaked paper towels filled the container. She smiled and thought, *Another experiment. I knew it!*

2

When Sylvia awoke the next morning, she could tell it was going to be a hot day in Philadelphia, even for the suburbs, where she lived. She had slept with the window open and the air felt heavy. No breeze came through the screen. She stretched and tried to make her toes touch the far end of the bed. Sylvia was sure she had grown at least an inch since the last day of school because she was now just about as tall as Kristen, who was an even five feet. In every other way, the girls were opposites. Sylvia had wavy hair like her mother, but it was much lighter, especially in the summer when it was streaked with blonde highlights. She wore it shoulder-length and parted to one side, and it was usually a little tousled. Her soft hazel eyes were framed with large, dark-rimmed glasses that she wore to see long distance. Her light skin burned easily, and it was sprinkled with freckles, which became more noticeable in the summer.

Kristen, on the other hand, had a dark-brown smooth complexion, large brown eyes with long lashes, and curly jet-black hair, which she kept short. Typically, she pulled it up in a small bun and wore different-colored headbands to keep it out of her way. Sylvia admired Kristen's clear skin and beautiful smile, compliments of two years of braces, which had just been removed. The one thing they had in common was their clothes, which they often shared, especially T-shirts with funny pictures or sayings.

Sylvia reached her right arm over her head to pull a tennis ball she had attached to a piece of string draped over her headboard. When she pulled the string down, it automatically lifted up the edge of an empty paper towel roll that had a marble inside. The marble rolled down the length of the paper towel roll and bumped into a larger ball sitting on the edge of Sylvia's desk. That ball was attached to a cord that controlled the window blinds. It rolled a few inches to the end of the desk, and as it fell off the edge, its weight pulled the cord, causing the blinds to roll up.

Sylvia smiled with satisfaction at her creation as the sunshine poured into her room. She loved summer because the days were so long. She lay in bed and let her mind wander, thinking about going to camp next week. When she and Kristen were in third grade, they had joined a Brownie troop where they were encouraged to learn about science. Their troop leader told them about a special camp called STEM, short for Science, Technology, Engineering, and Mathematics.

Going to STEM camp had been Sylvia's favorite part of the summer for the last two years. The days were filled with games and exciting experiments. They had even learned how to build a robot. Campers got to go on field trips and do fun activities like boating, swimming, and crafts. What Sylvia liked most was that she and Kristen attended together.

She rolled onto her side to look at the neat piles of items she planned to take to camp: shorts, shirts, socks, hiking shoes, swimsuit, goggles, camera, and a baseball cap. *I need sunscreen and a notepad*, she thought to herself. She hopped out of bed to search for the notepad, which should have been in her desk drawer. She searched the drawers, and under the desk and dresser without luck. *Where did I use it last?* she wondered. *The volcano! The kitchen!* She quickly changed her clothes, slipped on a T-shirt and shorts, ran a brush through her hair, and then headed down the steps toward the kitchen.

"Hi, Pumpkin Pie." Sylvia's dad greeted her with a smile in his voice.

"Good morning, Popsicle!" she replied.

"Good one," Mr. Petersen said, enjoying the game they played of swapping made-up names. "Mom is already out back in the garden. She wants you to help her with the weeding this afternoon."

"Okay, I'll do that right after I see Kristen."

"Make sure to eat something before you go, and brush your teeth!" Mr. Petersen was nearly a foot taller than Sylvia and had hazel-colored eyes, just like her. He was an engineer who worked for a company that manufactured medical equipment, and he shared Sylvia's love for science. He bent down and gave her a kiss on the forehead.

Sylvia went to the cupboard and selected three boxes. "Flakes, cinnamon squares, and pecan crunch," she announced, filling a bowl with equal parts of each. Then she carefully sliced half a banana on top and drenched the cereal with milk. She picked up the newspaper that her dad left on the kitchen table and looked at the headlines.

3D PRINTER HELPS TRAIN
BRAIN SURGEONS

Hmmm, Sylvia pondered. *Three-dimensional printing. Wow, I wonder if we could use that for our science project?* She tore out the article, folded it, tucked it into her back pocket, and then headed to the front door. Just above the doorknob was a yellow sticky note that read, BRUSH TEETH. Smiling, Sylvia ran upstairs to brush them, and then began walking to Kristen's, just a few blocks away.

3

"Come on in," Mrs. Dawson responded to Sylvia's three knocks on the door.

The door squeaked as Sylvia walked into the kitchen, where Kristen's mom was sitting at the table looking through a short stack of catalogues and magazines. Kristen sat next to her mother, wearing a bored expression.

"Hi, sweetie, how are you?" Mrs. Dawson asked.

"I'm good, thanks," Sylvia said. "What are you guys doing?"

"We're looking at the new fall fashion trends," Mrs. Dawson said, as she pointed to a picture of kids under the headline, BACK TO SCHOOL. "Just look at these rich colors and textured fabrics for the fall."

"Mom is trying to fix me," Kristen said flatly. "She thinks if I get new clothes, I'll be prettier and happier."

"Now, Kristen, you know that's not true," Mrs. Dawson corrected. "I think you are perfect just the way you are. I just think if you took a little more care in the way you dressed, you might like it."

"You mean you might like it, Mom."

"One pretty outfit won't hurt. Your sister loves getting new clothes."

"I'm not my sister. Besides, she's five years older than I am."

"Fine, we can do this later. But I'm sure Sylvia would love this outfit." Mrs. Dawson picked up a magazine displaying a teenage model wearing clothes that didn't resemble anything the girls had ever seen at their school.

Sylvia looked down at the orange flip-flops on her feet, jean shorts, and gray T-shirt. Her shirt featured an image of the periodic table of elements and the phrase, "I wear this shirt periodically." She looked back at the school-girl outfit in the magazine and answered, "Um, I don't really know a whole lot about fashion, but I guess it's really nice, Mrs. Dawson."

"We are going to be late!" Kristen bounced to her feet. "Mom, we gotta go."

"Late?" Mrs. Dawson looked puzzled. "Late for what? And where are you going?"

"Um—" Kristen exchanged glances with Sylvia, stalling for time as she tried to think up an acceptable answer. Finally she announced, "We are just going up to my room to work on that thing."

The three looked at each other awkwardly.

Kristen nudged Sylvia.

"Oh. Yes. That thing! That's right," Sylvia said. "We have that thing to work on to get ready for this year's science fair competition."

"Gotta go, Mom." Kristen gave her mom a quick kiss as the girls raced from the kitchen and up the front staircase to Kristen's room. Sylvia shut the door behind them, and they both jumped onto Kristen's bed, bouncing and laughing.

"What do you want to do?" Kristen asked.

"I don't know. We could do that 'thing!'" Sylvia said, teasing. She knew that Kristen had made that up so she could escape the fashion magazines.

"Well, since our volcano didn't exactly work out, we could actually try to think up a new experiment for the science fair."

Sylvia agreed. "Okay, let's go online."

Kristen hopped off the bed and grabbed her laptop. She placed it on the bed and flipped open the bright-green cover. The girls lay on their stomachs as they searched for interesting science experiments.

"Didn't you say you had an idea to build a rocket ship?" Sylvia asked.

"Yeah! Let's look it up."

"Here's one!"

"Cool," Kristen said. "If we got our volcano to explode, we could probably get a rocket to take off." The girls giggled and read with interest as they scrolled through a few pages of instructions.

"Which nose cone shape is most efficient on a rocket?" Sylvia read the text onscreen.

"Good question!" Kristen's interest grew. "We could make that into the perfect hypothesis."

By the third page, neither girl was smiling, and Kristen's eyes had glazed over.

Sylvia tried to get through some of the words. ". . . the nose cone introduces a second variable that you have to neutralize because of different shapes and volumes. If you multiply an object's volume by the material density, you get the object's weight. It can be challenging to separate the bulkhead disk into the tube and perpendicular to the sides . . ."

"What?" Kristen read the sentences over again and sighed. "Did that mean anything to you?"

"Not a thing," Sylvia admitted. "I'm thinking maybe it's a little too complicated for our first competition. Let's save that one for high school."

"Okay, the rocket experiment is off the list," Kristen agreed.

"We can probably get some great ideas at STEM camp next week."

"Umm, maybe." Kristen shrugged.

"What do you mean, maybe? Of course we'll get good ideas there," Sylvia said. She became animated. "Hey! Look what my mom got me!" She produced a round, shiny item from her pocket. "It's a compass. It's perfect for camp when we hike in the woods and get ourselves lost."

"Nice," Kristen replied politely.

"It's way more than nice, it's awesome!" Sylvia exclaimed. "Have you started packing yet?"

"Not yet."

"Why not? Want to start? I can help you."

"No."

"Why not?"

"I just don't, okay?" Kristen seemed irritated.

"Fine, I was just trying to help. What's the matter with you, anyway?"

"Nothing." She looked away and then blurted out, "Everything! I can't go to camp!"

"What do you mean, you can't go to camp?" Sylvia asked, as she looked at her friend in disbelief.

"I mean I can't go. My cousin Amelia is coming back home to get married, and my sister is in the wedding."

"So what? What does that have to do with you? Besides, I thought the wedding wasn't until this winter."

"Amelia got a scholarship to law school, so they moved the wedding up so they can get married before she starts school. It's in a few weeks, and my aunt asked my mom to help plan it. You know

15

how she lives for that kind of thing. We have to do all kinds of wedding stuff, like go to dress fittings and make party favors."

"Yuck!" Sylvia exclaimed.

"Double yuck." Kristen nodded. "It gets worse."

"How can it get worse?"

"Guess who my cousin is marrying?"

"Who?"

"Raj . . . Patel," Kristen said distinctly, pausing between the first and second names.

"Who is Raj Patel?" Sylvia asked. "The only Patel I know is Indra Patel."

Kristen remained silent as Sylvia's eyes grew wide.

"No, you mean Raj Patel is related to Indra Patel? The Indra Patel? The new girl? She is so annoying. Ever since she moved to our school last spring, you would think she owns it. Does she think about anything or anyone but herself? She doesn't even look at us, and she thinks we're geeks just because we're good at math and like science."

"We are geeks!"

"True." Sylvia laughed. "But that doesn't mean she has to be mean. I feel so bad for you. You are going to miss camp and have to spend time with her. I'll miss you so much!"

"I know, it stinks. Promise you're going to tell me what's happening every day, take pictures, and text me. I want to know everything."

"I promise," Sylvia said solemnly.

The girls each clapped their hands twice and then held up both hands toward each other to clap once with each other. They repeated two claps and then crossed their arms against their chests. It was a special handshake they had shared for years.

4

Mr. Petersen tossed Sylvia's duffle bag in the back of his SUV and closed the hatchback securely.

"That should do it!" he announced as he tapped the back of the car twice. Sylvia's bags were safely in place, and she was ready to head off to camp. Kristen had come over to see her off, and the two were talking excitedly.

"Did you remember your toothbrush?" Mrs. Petersen asked as she came out of the house.

"Yes," Sylvia replied.

"Did you pack enough underwear?"

"Yes."

"Did you remember dental floss?"

"Yes, Mom. I have enough floss for the entire camp. I think I've got everything covered. I'm only going to be gone for a couple of weeks."

"Let's go, Apple Pie," Mr. Petersen called out.

"Ready to go, Daddio!"

Mrs. Petersen put her arms around Sylvia and gave her a big hug. "Make sure to wear your sunscreen, eat enough, and don't stay up all night."

"Don't worry, Mom. I'll be fine." She rolled her eyes, but secretly loved that her mother worried about her.

Kristen stood next to Sylvia's mom, waiting to say good-bye. The girls hugged, and Kristen whispered, "I'll miss you."

"Me, too," Sylvia said. "I wish you were coming, and I'm so sorry you're stuck with all that wedding stuff."

Kristen agreed. "It's going to be awful."

"Hang in there!"

"I will. Have so much fun!"

Sylvia got into the car, fastened her seat belt, and waved.

"Good-bye!" she called out, as her dad backed the car out of the driveway.

Kristen and Mrs. Petersen waved until the car reached the end of the block and turned out of sight.

~ ~ ~

Two hours later, Sylvia and her father pulled into the campground.

"Look, Dad." Sylvia pointed excitedly at the camp sign. "We're here, we're here!" She quickly typed into her phone:

Just arrived!

Seconds later, Kristen texted back:

miss u have fun!

Mr. Petersen helped Sylvia unpack her bags and left an hour later. She joined about a hundred girls for lunch, followed by an orientation describing what was planned for the next two weeks. She was happy to see a few familiar faces from last year, and they had fun catching up on each other's news from the year. Together, they learned about what was in store for them at camp, which included learning about science, plus hiking, boating, archery, and swimming. The featured speaker was Patricia Woods, the head of engineering for the Department of the Navy stationed in Philadelphia.

Later that evening, Sylvia climbed to her second-level bunk bed and snuggled into her sleeping bag. She pulled out her phone to text Kristen.

S: *Great first day!*

As always, a reply appeared immediately:

K: ☺ *I miss you!*

S: *Our speaker is from the navy.*

K: *What's he do?*

S: *SHE is an engineer!*

K: *My bad. Cool!*

S: *We are going to a robotics competition!*

K: *So cool! Wish I was there!*

S: *Lights out–gotta go! Night*

K: *Bye*

Sylvia tucked her phone under her pillow, rolled over on her side, and quickly drifted off to sleep.

5

Sunlight streamed into the cabin and woke up Sylvia the next morning. She squinted to get her eyes used to the light, and then changed her mind and quickly closed them, trying to bury herself deeper into her sleeping bag. But it was too late. She was awake. It was still quiet in the cabin, so she lay in bed, waiting until the other girls woke up.

A vibration under her pillow startled her. Realizing it was her phone, Sylvia reached for it and pulled it out.

K: U up? she read, wondering why Kristen was awake so early.

S: Yes! Why are you up?

K: Going to a tea for the bride.

S: No way!

K: High tea!

S: Oh, no! That stinks!

K: Save meeee!!!

S: Ha ha . . . Good luck! ☺

Sylvia heard whispering and the creak of the floorboards under the feet of some of the girls who had climbed out of their bunks, so she decided to do the same. After unzipping her sleeping bag and scrambling down to the floor, she greeted the other girls as they got ready to go to the main event.

Sylvia's fellow campers ranged in age from twelve to fourteen. It was the first time she was there with the older girls, and she suddenly felt young, even though she would be turning 12 in just two weeks. She wondered if she would fit in, especially without Kristen. Her friend was so good at meeting other people, but Sylvia felt awkward on her own and found it difficult to make conversation. Everybody ate a breakfast of scrambled eggs and toast, and then they assembled under a large outdoor tent, where they sat on ten long benches facing a podium.

One of the camp leaders walked to the front and picked up a microphone to introduce the guest speaker:

"Patricia Woods is the head of engineering at the Navy Yard in Philadelphia. She manages all machinery related to ships and submarines. A scientific and engineering leader, Ms. Woods became the first woman to achieve the level of senior scientific technical manager in the navy. She graduated from the University of Pennsylvania with a bachelor of science degree and a master's degree in mechanical engineering. She has traveled on ships and aircraft carriers all over the world.

Please welcome Patricia Woods!"

The girls applauded as Ms. Woods walked toward the podium. Sylvia was amazed at her accomplishments. She thought someone who worked on ships would have to be big and tough looking, but she was wrong. Ms. Woods looked just like any of her friends' moms, except for the crisp navy blue pantsuit she wore.

"Good morning, girls," Ms. Woods greeted the crowd. "For some of you, this is the first time you are exploring the world of science, and for others, you have already discovered why science is so important. By the end of the week, I think you will all agree that science is not only important, but it's also exciting and fun!" Sylvia liked the warm tone of her voice and easy-going manner. She was impressed by how comfortable she appeared speaking in front of the large group, and wished she could project the same confidence as Ms. Woods did.

"Science enables us to learn about the world around us," Ms. Woods continued. "It helps us understand how our bodies work and how to heal them. Science gives us the tools we need to build bridges and skyscrapers. It provides the keys to unlock the world's mysteries.

"There have been many remarkable scientists throughout the years, and many have been women. But it hasn't always been that way. Less than a hundred years ago, most universities would not even allow women to graduate."

Ms. Woods went on to describe prominent women scientists, including **Mae Carol Jemison**, a chemical engineer, physician, and astronaut. She said that she was the first African-American woman to travel to space in the space shuttle Endeavor on September 12, 1992.

"**Maria Mitchell** was born in 1818 and grew up in Massachusetts, where she learned about the stars and navigation," explained Ms. Woods. "She later discovered a comet that was invisible to the naked eye, and she won a medal from the king of Denmark for her work. And she was the first woman elected to the American Academy of Arts and Sciences.

"**Elizabeth Blackwell** was the first woman to graduate from medical school in the United States. **Dr. Jane Goodall** became the world's foremost expert on chimpanzees and started a global nonprofit organization committed to conservation, safeguarding our planet, and respecting all living things. And **Barbara McClintock** was a pioneer in genetics, who won a Nobel Prize.

"All of these women helped pave the way for you and me to enter any scientific field we desire.

When I was young, I was very curious about how things worked, and I became excited to learn that science could help me understand how and why they worked. That's when I knew I wanted to work in the field of science. During the next two weeks, you will have the opportunity to explore many areas of science."

As Ms. Woods continued her speech, Sylvia imagined what her own future might hold. She smiled as she thought of the many possibilities.

The rest of the day was dedicated to activities that helped the girls get to know each other. Sylvia joined a group that went kayaking, and later everyone assembled for a cookout.

That evening during free time, Sylvia called her mom and dad, and then sent a text to Kristen, who must be so bored without her. Or so she thought.

S: *Hi!*
K: *Hi!* Kristen wrote back immediately.
Sylvia felt happy to connect.
S: *Camp is great! The speaker was awesome! We go see robotics tomorrow.*
K: *Fun!*
S: *Sorry you had to go to that silly tea party.*
K: *That's ok.*
S: *It must have been awful.*
K: *Not really.*

Not really? Sylvia stopped writing and thought about what to write back.

S: *But it was pretty bad, right?*

K: *IDK, it was sorta fun.*

Somehow, that's not what Sylvia wanted to hear. As she thought about what to say next, Kristen continued writing.

K: *Plaza Hotel in New York City was amazing.*

Sylvia felt a twinge of envy. They went all the way to New York? The girls had always talked about going to New York together. She responded:

S: *Long drive must have been tough.*

K: *We drove in a limo!!!*

Sylvia's heart sank. A limousine? Could it get any worse?

K: *Get this—Indra speaks two languages! Cool, right?*

S: *Sure.*

K: *G2G. Dinner. Shopping for wedding outfits tomorrow. Have fun at camp!*

S: *Will do.*

K: *Bye!*

S: *Cya.*

Sylvia felt a little rattled. She wanted to feel happy for Kristen, but somehow she couldn't. She comforted herself by thinking about tomorrow and the fun she would have learning about robotics.

Later that night, just before bed, Sylvia called Kristen. After four rings, she got Kristen's voice mail: "Hi, leave a message." Sylvia slouched in her sleeping bag and exhaled as she waited for the tone.

"Hi . . . it's me. Where are you? Call or text when you can." But no reply came for the rest of the night.

6

After breakfast the next day, the girls boarded buses and drove to Medford, New Jersey to attend a high school robotics competition. On the bus ride back to camp, Sylvia wrote a letter to her parents to tell them about her day.

Hi Mom and Daddio!

Today was unbelievable! We learned how to build a robot and watched kids control the ones they built to compete against each other in a game that took up an entire gym floor! It's called FIRST (For Inspiration and Recognition of Science and Technology). Ten high school teams were there. Everyone was cheering and music was playing, and the team we were rooting for won its match! It was like being at a football game, only not as cold! They have an actual competition season during school, so this match didn't count, but it was just as exciting.

The kids on the teams work on electronics, mechanics, even software, web design, and photography. The robots are about three feet tall and shaped like square metal boxes, like little file cabinets. They have moveable arms, and they can move all around the floor! Ours was named Robbie and was built by the team from Seneca High School in New Jersey. Robbie the Robot, ha ha! The team had to get Robbie to throw a ball into the other team's goal, and the other team tried to do the same thing with their robot. And they only had about two minutes to do it. It was so exciting! The students actually helped build everything, and then they let us try to control Robbie. It was amazing. I can't wait to be on a team when I get to high school. If you see Kristen, tell her I say hi!

Love,
Sylvia

Sylvia smiled at her letter as she recounted the excitement of the day, but her spirits were dampened because there was still no word from Kristen.

That evening, while she was walking to the recreation room to watch a movie with some of the girls, Sylvia felt a vibration in her pocket. It was Kristen calling! Since no phones were allowed during activities, she let the others know she would catch up with them in a minute. She listened to the phone message:

"Hey, Sylvia. Sorry I missed you. It's been really busy here. We spent all day shopping in town for the wedding. Then we had lunch. I had fondue. You have to try it! You dip food on sticks into melted cheese and chocolate. Even little pieces of cake! It was so much fun! I'll try and call again tomorrow, but Indra invited a bunch of girls to her country club to swim. Miss you, have fun."

Sylvia texted:

Today was epic! You would love it here. Shopping must have been exhausting, and that fondue thing sounds pretty messy. I thought you can't swim? Miss u 2.

Sylvia turned off her phone and ran to catch up with the other girls.

7

The next morning, Sylvia was surprised and relieved to see a text from Kristen waiting for her. Now she felt silly for feeling jealous.

Hey! Out all day, sleepover tonight. Talk tomorrow.

Sylvia stared at the message. Her breathing got heavier, and she could feel her heart pounding. *What is going on?* she wondered. She calmed herself and thought, *I'll be back at the end of next week and my birthday party is coming up. Kristen and I will have a blast, and everything will be back to normal.*

She turned off the phone, tucked it into a drawer, and focused on the day ahead. The girls were taking a field trip to the Academy of Natural Sciences in Philadelphia for the annual Bug Fest. The thought creeped Sylvia out. But she was excited to have a chance to talk with real scientists, learn about insects from all over the world, and cheer on a cockroach in the Roach Race 500! It was a famous bug race the Academy had held for years. Then, after dark, they would go to the nearby Franklin Institute to look at the night sky through powerful rooftop telescopes in their observatory. They would view stars, planets, and maybe even see a galaxy.

Each day at camp was filled with fun and interesting adventures, and she enjoyed meeting and spending time with other girls who shared her curiosity to learn new things. The girls had a chance to learn how to create software for video games, discover the chemistry behind almost every type of makeup, and find out how microscopic nanorobots could one day help people heal better and faster. Plus, when they weren't on a field trip, they had fun swimming in the lake and going on canoe rides, and making s'mores and telling stories around the campfire in the evenings.

But Sylvia felt a dark cloud hanging over her head. She had not heard back from Kristen, who seemed like she was always busy with Indra. Maybe now that she was going home, everything would get back to normal. She hoped so.

8

On Friday morning, the camp clubhouse was filled with chatter as the girls shared hugs and took their last photos of each other. A constant stream of minivans filed by and picked up campers. Sylvia's spirits lifted when her parents' red Jeep pulled up to the curb. Her mom and dad were just opening the car doors when she reached them. Mrs. Petersen hugged her, and then Sylvia ran around the car to meet her dad.

"Hi, Superstar!" her dad called out as he picked her up off the ground a few inches and squeezed her in a bear hug.

Sylvia talked nonstop on the ride home, describing every day in detail. As they finally pulled into the driveway, her old white two-story house with a wraparound porch was a welcome sight. Sylvia admired the yard filled with colorful flowers her mother had planted. Her favorites were the pale-blue hydrangeas, which were starting to turn brown—the first sign that summer was coming to a close. She hated to think of the season ending, but it meant her birthday was coming. In fact, her party was tomorrow!

Each year, Sylvia looked forward to her birthday

and doing something special. Last year, she and Kristen and their mothers went to see *The Lion King* musical in Philadelphia and had a big lunch, followed by a family party and a sleepover. This year, she was allowed to invite friends to Great Adventure amusement park. She and Kristen planned to ride every roller coaster. She also invited two of the girls from her Girl Scout troop, who were neighbors. Lindsey and Lauren were twin sisters, one year younger than Sylvia. They had all grown up playing with each other after school.

"Mom, when we get home, can I go see Kristen?"

"After you unpack and put your dirty clothes in the wash," her mom replied. "And, I want you home by five."

"Okay."

As soon as the car came to a stop, Sylvia grabbed her duffle bag and backpack and raced up the steps to her room. After dumping the contents of her bag onto her bed, she ran to the laundry room for a basket and returned to the mound of crumpled clothes. Wrapping her arms around the pile as if she were giving it a big hug, she stuffed it all into the basket. Then she shoved her full backpack into her closet where she hoped her mom wouldn't see it.

"Done!" Sylvia announced out loud, although she knew her mother would never approve of her lackluster cleanup effort.

Sylvia went downstairs and called to her mom, "I'm going now!"

"Did you unpack?"

"Yes!"

"Are you sure?"

"Um, pretty sure." Sylvia held her breath, hoping her mom wouldn't check her room and keep her home.

"Okay, be home by five," her mom called out.

"Okay, see you soon!" she called back with relief.

Sylvia arrived at Kristen's home ten minutes later. She knocked on the door and cracked it open, calling out, "Hello!"

Mrs. Dawson responded, "Hello?"

"It's me, Sylvia!"

"Hi, sweetie, come on in. I'm in the family room."

Sylvia walked through the kitchen and into the family room, where she found Mrs. Dawson sitting on the floor surrounded by boxes, bags, and spools of ribbon.

"I'm making favors for the wedding. Aren't they pretty?" Mrs. Dawson asked, as she held one up for Sylvia to admire.

Sylvia tried to make sense of the party favors that appeared to be some type of candy wrapped in white netting, tied up with light-blue ribbon, and decorated with delicate sprigs of fake flowers.

She wasn't quite sure what she thought of the creation, but politely replied, "Yes," though it sounded more like a question than a statement.

"This has been so much fun preparing for the wedding," Mrs. Dawson exclaimed. "I can't believe it's finally here. I just love weddings, don't you?"

"I guess so." Sylvia shrugged. "I've never really been to one. Is Kristen in her room?"

"No, honey, she's not home."

"Oh." Sylvia's voice showed her surprise and her spirits sank.

"Was she expecting you?"

"Kind of," Sylvia said. "She knew I was coming home from camp today, and I thought we were going to hang out. I guess she forgot."

"Oh, I'm sorry, Sylvia. Kristen has been so busy with all the wedding fun, she probably did forget."

"That's okay," Sylvia replied. "When will she be home?"

"She's at the club swimming with Indra and her friends right now, and then we are all having dinner there. I just love the club. The people are so nice and interesting. Maybe you girls can get together tomorrow after the shower."

"Shower?" Sylvia frowned.

"Mrs. Patel is hosting a wedding shower at the club tomorrow for twenty guests. I can only guess how expensive it will be. I'm sure I don't have the right thing to wear."

Sylvia really wasn't listening as Mrs. Dawson worried about her outfit. Tomorrow was her birthday party! There must be some mistake.

"What time is the shower over?" Sylvia asked.

"I don't know," Mrs. Dawson replied. "I suppose we will have brunch, play some games, and watch my niece open presents. I wonder what they will be serving. No doubt it will be elegant. Mrs. Patel does everything first class."

Sylvia stared blankly at Mrs. Dawson as she continued to talk on and on about the shower.

"Sorry, honey. There I go, rambling about the wedding plans. Do you want me to have Kristen call you after the shower? I'm sure she will want to tell you all about it."

"Sure, thanks," Sylvia murmured. "I guess I'll get going."

Sylvia could feel tears starting to pool in her eyes. She didn't want to hear about the wedding shower. She wanted to tell Kristen all about camp. Had she actually forgotten her birthday party?

9

"Oh . . . my . . . gosh, Kristen! You look so cute!" Indra said, admiring Kristen's sun hat. "Doesn't she look adorable?" Indra asked her friends, Nicole and Judy.

"Absolutely adorable!" Nicole confirmed with a distinctive nod of her head.

"Thank you." Kristen was flattered by all the attention.

The four girls had spent most of the last two weeks together. Nicole and Judy were Indra's two closest friends. Kristen knew them from school, but they had never spoken to her before. She was excited to be with them, relaxing on lounge chairs around the pool at the club Indra's family belonged to. Indra was looking at fashion blogs on her iPad, and the other girls browsed through fashion magazines and talked about everything and everybody. Kristen was surprised by how much the girls gossiped about the other kids at school. She felt it wasn't very nice, but she couldn't help listening and reacting to everything the girls said. She loved being around this popular group of girls.

"Look how pretty this scarf is." Judy held up a

picture from her magazine.

"It's pretty," Indra agreed. "The design reminds me of a sari that I saw at a wedding last year."

"What's a 'sorry'?" Kristen asked.

"A 'sari' is sort of a dress that women wear in India," Indra explained. "It's a very long and wide strip of fabric that drapes around your body into an outfit. There are different styles for every region in India."

"Wow, how do you know all of that?"

"Because my grandparents are from India," Indra replied. "I'm named after my grandmother."

"That's cool. Will your mom be wearing a sari at the wedding?"

"No, she doesn't follow many of the Indian traditions," Indra continued. "She says that in the old days, girls didn't have as much of an opportunity to get an education or have a career. But now my mom is all about her career and making sure that she joins the right clubs, and that my sister and I get into the best colleges."

"She's already planning your college?" Kristen laughed.

"Yep, it's no joke," Indra said. "She makes sure we look right, act right, and get the grades."

The girls all looked serious, and Indra suddenly felt uncomfortable with the attention.

"But hey, that's not hard to do when it's me!"

she said quickly, to lighten the conversation.

"Isn't this outfit adorable?" Nicole called out as she held up a page from her magazine for the girls to admire.

"Adorable," Indra said. "You should so definitely wear that for the first day of school, Kristen."

"Definitely," Nicole said as Judy nodded in approval.

"Do you really think so?" Kristen hesitated as she looked at the expensive price noted on the page.

"You can get it when we all go shopping on Monday," Indra announced. "I just love back-to-school shopping."

"Sounds like fun." Kristen smiled halfheartedly, as she wondered how she could possibly afford such an outfit. She would have to spend a month of babysitting money.

~~~

Later, after loading up on frozen yogurt at the snack bar, Indra asked about her friend Danielle, who was supposed to come hang out at the pool with the girls.

"Oh, I guess she didn't tell you," Nicole said with an air of importance.

"Tell me what?" Indra sat up and looked intently at Nicole.

"Danielle told me she couldn't come today

because she had some kind of Girl Scout thing!" Nicole announced.

"She's twelve and still in Girl Scouts? Can you believe it?" Indra asked dramatically.

"I know, how lame." Nicole shrugged.

Twelve! Oh, my gosh, Kristen thought. *Sylvia's twelfth birthday is tomorrow!* She had completely forgotten. Her mind raced as she tried to think of what she should do, realizing she would miss Sylvia's birthday party because she had to go to her cousin's wedding shower instead.

"Right, Kristen?" Indra's voice startled her.

"What?" Kristen had been caught off guard.

"Can you believe Danielle LaRosa is still in Girl Scouts?" Indra repeated.

Kristen thought of all the fun she had in Girl Scouts and the nice girls she met over the years.

"I think it's okay if Danielle is still in Girl Scouts," Kristen replied.

Judy and Nicole looked at Kristen in disbelief. No one disagreed with Indra. Nicole's mouth dropped open in shock.

Kristen corrected herself. "For some people, that is. But not for me."

"Definitely," Nicole said, and they went on chatting.

Kristen felt bad that she had lied, but she didn't want to say anything that would keep the girls from liking her. She also felt guilty for forgetting Sylvia's birthday. Sliding her phone out of her pool bag, she hid it under her beach towel and sent a text to Sylvia.

K: *OMG Happy Birthday* ☺
   So sorry I can't be there tomorrow!!!

Just a minute later, a response came back:

S: *r u?*
K: *I don't have a choice . . .*
S: *no big*
K: *don't be like that!*
S: *like what? I'm fine*
K: *I'll make it up to you! Promise!*
S: *just forget it*

10

The next morning, Sylvia woke up and reached her right arm over her head to tug on the tennis ball and make the blinds go up. They revealed dreary weather, which matched her mood. She decided it was a sign that her birthday was going to be a disaster. She shuffled into the bathroom to splash her face and took a long look in the mirror. Her hair was tousled. The sun had created threads of golden highlights, making it appear lighter than usual. Her nose and cheeks were pink from the sun, and freckles had sprouted across her nose. *Twelve,* she thought. *I'm almost a teenager and I'm going to start middle school.* Somehow it seemed like a new phase of her life was starting. Sylvia glanced at her phone, but there were no messages. She picked it up to write Kristen a message, changed her mind, tossed the phone on her bed and headed down the stairs. *What's the use?* she thought.

A handmade sign with the words HAPPY BIRTHDAY drawn in blue block letters followed by an arrow pointing toward the kitchen greeted Sylvia at the bottom of the steps. Her spirits lifted as she entered the kitchen, where her mother waited with a plate piled high with blueberry pancakes. She smiled at her mother and snuggled into her arms for a big hug, and then sat down and dug her fork into the delicious mound of steaming pancakes.

"There are a few cards on the counter for you that came in the mail," Mrs. Petersen announced.

"Can I open them now?" Sylvia questioned through a mouthful of pancakes. Then she got up to retrieve the cards before her mom had a chance to respond.

She opened the first of the cards. "This one is from MomMom and PopPop, with a check for twenty-five dollars!"

She ripped into the next one, which was from her aunt and uncle, and then looked at the last card that only had her name written on the outside. Sylvia recognized Kristen's handwriting and slid the card unopened under the other two.

"What time are we leaving for Great Adventure?" she asked her mom.

"Lauren and Lindsey will be here in thirty minutes, so you better get ready to go," Mrs. Petersen replied.

Sylvia picked up her cards and ran upstairs to get ready for the day ahead.

~~~

Later that night, Mrs. Petersen tapped on Sylvia's door to say goodnight. She found her already in bed, looking at a large picture book of astronomy.

"Hi, birthday girl, I came to say goodnight," her mother whispered. "Did you have a good time today?"

"I really did, Mom. I think we rode every roller coaster twice. I had so much fun with Lauren and Lindsey, and the cake you made me was awesome!"

"I'm sorry Kristen couldn't make it today. I know you were disappointed."

"It doesn't matter, Mom." Sylvia shrugged. "If she's too busy for me, then I don't really care."

"Everything will work out, sweetie," her mother said comfortingly.

"Sure, Mom. Thanks again for a great day."

Mrs. Petersen kissed Sylvia on the forehead and left her room. Sylvia closed her book and placed it on the nightstand. She opened the top drawer and pulled out a small stack of birthday cards and picked up the one from Kristen. She opened the envelope to reveal a handmade card. She read, *Happy birthday, Sylvia! I'm so sorry I had to miss your big day. I promise I'll make it up to you.*

Sylvia let out a soft sigh, shoved the cards back into the drawer, and turned out the light.

11

A week passed and Sylvia still hadn't communicated with Kristen. The wedding had taken place over the weekend, and Sylvia hoped life could finally return to normal. But even when she tried to stop thinking about it, she saw wedding pictures splashed across the society section of the newspaper. Now, on the first day of school, Sylvia was looking forward to starting a new routine. She put on her favorite blue shirt and a pair of khaki shorts. She slid a leather belt through the loops of her shorts and put on a pair of sneakers, a birthday gift from her aunt.

For the first time, Sylvia walked to school alone. She missed sharing the anticipation of the first day of middle school with Kristen.

When Sylvia arrived, students were hanging out in small groups outside the school, laughing and talking about summer vacations. Sylvia searched the sea of faces to find Kristen and finally spotted her standing near the front steps with Indra. She walked toward her friend and waved to attract her attention. But Kristen seemed to be smiling at someone behind her. Turning, Sylvia watched as Judy and Nicole passed her by and embraced

Kristen with loud squeals of delight. Suddenly, Sylvia felt out of place with the girl who was supposed to be her best friend.

"Hi," Sylvia said to Kristen when she reached the group of girls.

"Hi," Kristen replied hesitantly.

"Are we okay?" Sylvia asked.

"Yeah, of course," Kristen smiled. Sylvia felt a wave of relief.

The other girls glanced at her without saying anything and resumed their conversation. Sylvia felt painfully awkward while she waited for Kristen to introduce her, but she never did.

"Hi, I'm Sylvia," she finally sputtered out.

Indra stopped talking and looked at her, as the other girls followed her lead. Fidgeting with a braided bracelet on her left wrist, Sylvia felt their gazes as though they judged her outfit from head to toe.

"Hi," Indra said indifferently, and then continued talking to the other girls.

"Kristen, are you excited for honors math?" Sylvia pressed on, but got no response.

"You look pretty," Sylvia finally said as she admired Kristen's skirt.

"Thanks, it's a couture piece," Kristen replied.

"Oh." Sylvia had no idea what that meant.

Indra's ears perked up when she heard the girls

discussing fashion.

"The minute we saw that skirt, we just knew Kristen had to have it," Indra explained. "She looks adorable, right?"

"Definitely," Judy said.

"Definitely," Nicole said. "It cost a small fortune."

"We should go shopping this weekend to celebrate our first week of school!" Indra announced.

"Definitely," Nicole and Judy said in unison.

The girls looked toward Kristen and waited for her reply.

"Oh, sure . . . definitely," she obediently chimed in.

Sylvia's eyes grew wide in disbelief, and she tried to change the subject.

"Are you going to first-period honors science?" Sylvia asked Kristen.

"Yes," Kristen nodded.

"What a drag," Indra exclaimed. "I can't believe I have to take that class. My parents insisted that I need it if I'm ever going to go to the right college and be 'someone.' Just like my brother, the doctor, and my sister, who is going to be a lawyer. And, according to my mother, I am going to be . . . a big disappointment. It's all about grades. They are obsessed. How lame, right?"

Judy agreed. "So lame. I'm glad I'm not in that class."

"Definitely lame," Nicole chimed in. "No way. I'm not taking honors anything."

"You want to walk over together?" Sylvia asked Kristen.

"You go ahead, Cindy," Indra said, "we'll see you there."

Sylvia looked at Kristen, who shrugged.

"I guess I'll see you there." Sylvia turned away, trying not to look hurt.

12

That Indra is bad news, Sylvia thought as she marched off to class by herself. *I'll fix that.* Sylvia got to class early and picked a seat near the front, saving the seat behind her for Kristen. When Kristen finally appeared with Indra, Sylvia waved her over, but she filed right past her to seats in the back row. *What is going on?* Sylvia wondered.

"Welcome, honors science students." Mrs. Carter's voice boomed with enthusiasm. "We have students from both seventh and eighth grades, but you all have one thing in common . . . a love of science. And you will have your chance to learn a lot in this class, because I say the sky is the limit!"

Sylvia listened intently with a feeling of excitement, while in the back of the room, Indra rolled her eyes and doodled on her notepad.

"Let's get right to the point today and talk about what I know is on everyone's minds," Mrs. Carter continued. "I know many of you have been thinking about the science fair competition. If you aren't already aware, our science fair is about exploring any aspect of science that is of interest to you. That could be chemistry, engineering, astronomy, physics, biology, and more."

Mrs. Carter passed out guideline sheets to explain. "You are challenged to create an experiment that uses the scientific method to demonstrate the use of scientific principles." She pointed to a chart on the wall that listed the steps in the method:

o **Ask a Question**
o **Conduct Research**
o **Form a Hypothesis (predict what will happen)**
o **Test the Hypothesis by Doing an Experiment**
o **Analyze the Outcome (data)**
o **Draw a Conclusion**
o **Communicate the Results**

"And remember, in order to make your experiment a fair test, you have to change only one variable and keep everything else the same. Let's use an example." Mrs. Carter pointed to each word on the chart and continued her explanation:

"**Question:** *I wonder what food product keeps ants away the best?*

"**Research:** *Look for information in the library, or on the Internet, or conduct interviews to learn more.*

"**Hypothesis:** *Based on what you have learned, form a hypothesis.* Your hypothesis might be, 'I think citrus fruits will keep ants away.'

"**Experiment:** *Remember to make a fair experiment.* You can change just one variable each time you test it. You might place a specific number of ants in a box, on one side of a line drawn down the middle. Then, put little pieces of food, such as coffee grinds, lemon rinds, and garlic on the other side of the line, to see if the ants cross for the food. You will change only one variable, the food, to test the ants' reaction.

"**Analysis:** *Review the data you collect.* How many ants crossed the line for each food product?

"**Conclusion and Communicate:** *Determine which food product kept ants away best and report on the outcome.*

"That's a simple example of how to approach your experiments," Mrs. Carter concluded. "We will work together to learn more over the next few weeks. You may choose to work on your own or form a team of up to three people. You will be judged on how innovative or original your project is, how it utilizes science principles, and how well you present it in front of the audience and judges. Each team will have ten minutes to present their experiments."

Sylvia shifted in her seat and made a row of exclamation points after the instruction about presenting in front of the class.

"Any questions?" her teacher asked.

Sylvia raised her hand.

"Yes?"

"Does everyone on the team have to speak?" Sylvia asked.

"Yes, everyone has to take part in the presentation."

Sylvia's heart sank as she recalled the last time she had made a presentation for a project. Her assignment in history class was to report on a famous woman. She loved reading and researching about Marie Curie, a physicist and chemist who conducted research on radioactivity and was the first woman to win a Nobel Prize in 1903. Sylvia knew everything about her and had memorized every word of her report, but when she stood in front of her classmates her mind went completely blank. Her mother called it being tongue-tied, and that's exactly what it felt like. She remembered searching from face to face for encouragement but found none. The color rose in her cheeks and she was overcome with embarrassment. She couldn't bear to do that again!

Sylvia made a mental note to tell Kristen that she would have to be in charge of the presentation. Kristen was so good at speaking, and that would give Sylvia confidence. The girls had been waiting for their chance to compete in the fair, and they hoped to win it the first year of middle school. No seventh grader had ever done that before.

With fifteen minutes remaining in class, Mrs. Carter announced that the students could form their teams for the competition. Sylvia made her way to the back to connect with Kristen.

"This is going to be good, but you have to do most of the talking because there is no way I'm speaking in front of class," Sylvia said to Kristen.

"Well, about that . . ." Kristen hesitated.

Sylvia interrupted. "No, you have to do most of the talking."

Kristen looked away uncomfortably, and then turned to Sylvia and said, "I'm not really sure that's going to work out."

"What do you mean?"

Indra appeared behind Sylvia and listened to the girls' conversation with interest.

"Well . . . since Indra transferred schools, this is all new to her, and she asked me to be in a group with her."

Indra glanced at Sylvia, cocked her head to one side, and shrugged as if to say, *Too bad for you*.

"What?" Sylvia looked at both girls' faces and realized that she would have to invite Indra to join their group.

She composed herself and said, "That's okay, Indra can be part of our team."

"How sweet of you, Olivia," Indra said flatly. "But I'm sorry, we already have three in our group." She tapped Max on the shoulder and continued. "Max is so creative and such a good artist. He said he could design all the posters and charts for our presentation. Isn't that sweet of him?" she gushed, and Max blushed. "Sorry, Olivia," she said with such pity that it made Sylvia's blood boil.

"It's Sylvia!" she blurted out. "Don't think I don't know exactly what's going on here." She spun on her heel to leave.

"Wait! Don't be mad," Kristen called out, walking quickly after her. "You're so good at science, you'll be fine. Indra is new to all this, so I can help her."

"Oh, and Max? You don't even know him, but it sure sounds like he will come in handy putting your presentation together. She's using you, Kristen. She's using you both."

"It's not like that."

"Oh, really?" Sylvia pushed on. "We've been planning to do a project together for a year. You know I can't do the presentation myself. This ruins everything!"

"Sorry. Please don't be mad."

The sign-up list for teams had filled up by the time Sylvia got to it, and she realized she would have to do the project alone.

The ping of a bell signaled the end of class. It came as welcome relief to Sylvia. Maybe she could smooth things over at lunch. The girls typically took their lunches to school in bags and often shared each other's food. This would be the first time they could really talk and patch things up. Sylvia saw Kristen already seated at a table and walked over to join her.

"Hey, Sylvia," Kristen said brightly. "Why don't you eat with us?" She motioned to Indra, Judy, and Nicole.

"Who is us?"

Kristen ignored the response as Sylvia sat down across from her and unwrapped her sandwich.

"How quaint," Indra said, nodding to Sylvia's tuna sandwich.

"What happened, did you forget your lunch and have to buy?" Sylvia asked Kristen.

"No, I just thought I would buy lunch this year," Kristen said.

"Nobody brings their lunch in middle school," Indra announced as she raised her eyebrows.

"Guess I'm nobody, then," Sylvia said, and took a big bite of her sandwich. "Boy, Kristen, you missed so much at science camp."

"What is science camp?" Indra was suddenly curious.

"It's a two-week camp that focuses on a variety

of careers in science," Sylvia explained. "Our Girl Scout leader told us about it. It's so cool!"

"Girl Scouts?" Indra acted shocked.

"Kristen and I have been in the same troop for years."

"How sweet," Indra replied. "And you are a Girl Scout, too, Kristen?"

Judy and Nicole stopped talking and watched intently to see what would happen next.

The color started to rise in Kristen's cheeks. "I used to be, but not anymore."

"Used to be?" Sylvia asked. She could feel her breathing getting heavier. "Since when did you quit?"

"Since a while ago." Kristen, her face reddening further, half-smiled at her new friends.

Sylvia hastily packed up her sandwich and blurted out to Kristen, "What is the matter with you?" She turned and left before the girls could see her cry.

"What's her problem?" Judy asked out loud.

"Where's the geek patrol?" Indra asked, and Judy and Nicole joined her in laughter.

Kristen tried to join in with a smile, but knew she had hurt Sylvia's feelings with her lie. That was the price she would have to pay if she wanted to be a part of her new group of friends.

13

Sylvia's walk home from school was slow and sad. Every other year, she couldn't wait to tell her mom about her day and then recount it later with Kristen. But today was different. She didn't want to remember anything.

As Sylvia neared Kristen's house, she spotted her friend getting out of Indra's family car. Quickly, she tried to duck out of sight behind a bush.

"Hey, I can still see you," Kristen called out.

Sylvia came out from behind the shrub and confronted her friend. "I didn't see you after lunch. You weren't in math class. What happened?"

"Oh, about that. It turns out I had to drop out of honors math."

"Why? You were top in the class last year!"

"Math really isn't that cool, Sylvia. Think about it. We're already taking honors science. No reason to be total geeks. Besides, it's at the same time as video production class, and that sounds so exciting!"

"You couldn't even figure out how to take a picture of our volcano. Suddenly you think it's so great?"

"Indra says video is hot right now, so we are all

taking it together."

"We?"

"Yeah, Indra and our friends."

"You've changed," Sylvia snapped. "You're dressing crazy, acting crazy, and your new 'friend,'" she said, making imaginary quotation marks with her fingers, "is using you to win the science competition."

"That's not fair," Kristen said defensively. "Indra is so much fun, and the girls really like me."

"No, they like the person you are pretending to be, not the person you are."

"Did you ever stop to think that I might like stuff that's different from what you like, and that's okay? Everything doesn't have to be about you." Kristen swung her backpack over her shoulder.

"You've made that pretty clear because you're making sure that nothing is about me, so I hope you're happy."

"I'm very happy."

"Good."

"Good."

Both girls stomped off in opposite directions.

14

The next Friday after school, Sylvia's mother found her reading a book and eating an apple at the kitchen counter. She greeted her with a kiss on the head.

"Hi, Mom," Sylvia said without looking up.

"Do you think we can try that again with a little more enthusiasm?"

"Hi, Mom," Sylvia said a little louder. She looked up and then went back to her book.

"Aren't you going over to the carnival at the elementary school this evening? You always used to love that."

Each year the school held a carnival featuring games and food booths to raise money for the school.

"No," Sylvia replied. "I'm pretty sure I've outgrown that."

"I see. Do you want to talk about it?"

"What do you mean by that?" Sylvia asked.

"I'm thinking something is bothering you," Mrs. Petersen replied.

"There's really nothing to say." Sylvia returned to her book, but realized she had been reading the same paragraph over and over.

"Okay," Mrs. Petersen said. "I'll just start dinner while you read." She began to take some items out of the refrigerator and set them on the counter.

Sylvia took a loud bite out of her apple, and her eyes glistened with tears as she looked at her mom. Still chewing, her words came tumbling out.

"Kristen is acting like she has been taken over by aliens. She's wearing all these cool clothes. I think she is even wearing eyeliner. There's this girl, Indra. Everyone does whatever she says. I'm just about the only girl left in honors math. And I have to do the science fair by myself. I'm a loser, Mom, no one likes me, and I hate school."

"Well, that seems like a little more than nothing to talk about," Sylvia's mom said, her knife poised above the carrots.

Sylvia blew her nose into her napkin and then started crying again. Mrs. Petersen handed her another napkin, and then asked, "Should I get a roll of paper towels?" Sylvia smiled and her tears turned into a combination of crying and laughter as her mom embraced her.

"Sometimes there's nothing like a good cry." Mrs. Petersen blotted away the final tears on Sylvia's cheeks.

"I really don't know why I'm crying."

"Sounds like you are a little frustrated at school and with your friends. But that was a pretty long

61

list of problems. Shall we start with why you hate school?"

"I guess I really don't hate school," Sylvia confessed. "But it doesn't seem like much fun anymore."

"And the part about no friends? I, for one, know you have a lot of friends."

"I know I have friends. It just seems like someone flicked a switch and I don't even know Kristen anymore. She dropped honors math because she says everyone is taking video instead."

"People change at different times and in different ways," Mrs. Petersen said. "I'm not saying Kristen isn't behaving a little strangely, like you say, but did you ever think that you are the one who isn't open to changing?"

"They're making me feel stupid, Mom."

"Trust me, Sylvia, you are not stupid." Mrs. Petersen smiled. "I know sometimes people say cruel things and hurt our feelings. You know what Eleanor Roosevelt once said? 'No one can make you feel inferior without your consent.' She was the First Lady of the United States, so she knew a thing or two about facing criticism. She was also a supporter of human rights and women's issues."

"Are you saying it's my fault that I feel bad?"

"No, I'm saying you can either let other people make you feel bad and do what they want you to do, or you can do what is right for you, and be proud of it."

"So I should stay in math if I really love it, and not just take video class because everybody else is?" Sylvia questioned.

"Exactly. I think you will discover who your true friends are. But first you have to be true to yourself. They will find their way, and so will you."

"I guess I knew that. But I still don't have anyone to do the science project with."

"I thought you and Kristen were working on an idea."

"We were, but she decided to work with Indra. It's like I'm out and she's in."

Mrs. Petersen sighed. "That's a tough one. You know, when it comes to people who don't seem to be doing the right thing, it's nice to give them a chance, but it's also a good idea to trust your gut."

She kissed Sylvia on the head and returned to making dinner. Sylvia wasn't exactly sure what her mom meant about trusting her gut, but she decided to go up to her room and start putting together a science project anyway. Even if Kristen wouldn't be there to help her present it, Sylvia knew she could come up with an idea.

But an hour later, she still had nothing. She heard the door close and went to the front hall to greet her father.

"Hi, Dad."

"Just 'Dad'?" Do I detect someone isn't in a good mood?"

"Just a serious mood," Sylvia replied. "I can't seem to come up with an idea for a science experiment."

"I find that highly unusual," Mr. Petersen laughed.

"It's not funny, Dad." Sylvia showed no hint of a smile. "I'm all dried up. No ideas. Nothing. Nada."

"How can I help?" Her dad took his coat off and hung it up.

"I don't know," she replied glumly.

Her dad motioned to the stairs and they both sat.

After a minute of silence her dad suggested, "Maybe the best thing is to think of a problem, and then think about how you could fix it."

"Like what kind of a problem?" Sylvia asked.

"I don't know," her dad continued. "Like my problem is how can I make my coffee taste better?"

"I don't exactly think that's a science experiment."

"Well, maybe your mom has a problem. What does she want to solve?"

"I don't know, maybe how to grow her plants better in the garden."

"Okay." Her dad encouraged her. "What variables are there?"

"I guess temperature, soil, light, water." Sylvia made a mental list. "This could work. I bet I could look at one of those and test different variables!"

"Sounds like a science experiment in the making." Mr. Petersen sounded pleased with himself.

"Awesome, Dad, you are brilliant!" Sylvia announced with renewed enthusiasm. She gave him a quick peck on the cheek, jumped up, and headed up the stairs. "Gotta go and write a hypothesis!"

Plants, she thought, once she was in her room. *Light, water, temperature, what could make them grow better or differently? I don't know. I don't think I know what I'm doing. I wonder what's on TV.*

She started pacing back and forth, until she stopped in front of her window and stared outside. A light caught her eye, and she realized she was seeing the setting sun's rays bounce off the stained glass of the church windows a few blocks away. She admired how the colored light danced on the glass. *I wonder if colored light is the same as regular light*, Sylvia thought. *I wonder if things can grow in colored light or maybe even better than regular light. I wonder if they grow at all in colored light.*

"That's it!" she exclaimed. "Does the color of

light have an effect on plant growth?" She realized
she had figured out her experiment!

15

On Monday morning, Sylvia saw Lauren and Lindsey from the neighborhood, and they walked to school together talking about school, Girl Scouts, and Great Adventure. Sylvia had to admit to herself that she did have a good time at the amusement park, even though she wished Kristen had been there. When they reached the elementary school, the girls parted ways because the younger girls were in sixth grade, which was in a separate building. Sylvia continued to the middle school on her own, arriving just as Indra's family car pulled up. Indra, Kristen, Judy, and Nicole stepped out and walked up the school steps like models on a runway. Each had a different-colored scarf wrapped around her neck. Sylvia remembered Eleanor Roosevelt's quote, *No one can make you feel inferior without your consent.* She took a deep breath, stood straighter, and marched to science class.

Mrs. Carter reminded the students that proposals for their projects were due on Friday. Sylvia did her best to avoid making eye contact with Kristen and Indra. Later, dreading going to lunch, Sylvia hoped she would not run into

Kristen. But it was Indra who saw Sylvia first.

Oh boy, here comes trouble, Sylvia thought, but she was surprised to see Indra waving her over.

"Sylvia, I think we got off to a bad start, and I really want to fix that," Indra said.

"You know my name?" Sylvia said with surprise.

"Of course I do, silly. Why don't you sit with us today?"

"Okay," Sylvia said cautiously.

Sylvia sat down and unwrapped a turkey sandwich, while Indra, Judy, and Nicole ate chicken wraps from their trays.

"Where's Kristen?" Sylvia asked.

"She's in the library," Indra replied. "Your sandwich looks yummy."

"Oh, thanks," Sylvia replied, wondering why she wasn't being teased for bringing her lunch to school. "We had turkey for dinner on Sunday."

"So, everyone thinks you're really good at science," Indra continued. "I really admire that."

"You do?" Sylvia felt disbelief.

"Sure." Indra smiled. "I think science is so hard. I'm really sorry we couldn't be on a team together."

"You are?"

"Oh yes, really." Indra's tone was reassuring.

Sylvia found herself counting the number of times Indra said really.

"Do you have an idea for the science fair yet?"

"I do," Sylvia responded enthusiastically. "I've been working on something special."

"That's really great! I'm so excited for you. What's it about?"

"You honestly want to hear about it?" Sylvia was thrilled.

"Yes, I'm fascinated. Tell us all about it."

Sylvia could hardly contain her enthusiasm as she described her idea to test the effect of different colors of light on the growth of plants. She detailed her hypothesis and how she would set up the experiment. She was surprised that Indra hung on every word. For the first time, she left lunch period with a happy heart. Maybe she had been wrong about Indra. Maybe she just had to give her a chance.

The whole week went better, and Indra even waved to her in the halls. On Wednesday, Indra greeted her in science class, and on Thursday she told Sylvia that she liked her T-shirt.

Every evening Sylvia worked on finalizing her science fair proposal, and by Friday she was ready to turn it in. She proudly placed her proposal on Mrs. Carter's desk as soon as she walked into the classroom.

At the end of class, Mrs. Carter looked at Sylvia with a concerned expression and asked, "Sylvia, will you come by my desk before you leave, please?"

"Yes," Sylvia replied, picking up her notebook.

"It's about your science fair proposal. It's very similar to a proposal I received and approved earlier this week."

"I don't understand."

"Actually, I don't understand," Mrs. Carter said. "If I didn't know you were such a good student, I might have thought you copied it from another group that submitted a proposal on Wednesday."

She held up a proposal from Indra, Kristen, and Max.

Sylvia's eyes grew wide, and her mouth hung open as she stared at the page titled, THE EFFECT LIGHT COLOR HAS ON PLANT GROWTH. Sylvia hardly noticed what her teacher was saying because all she could hear was the sound of her pounding heart. *How could they betray me?*

"I'll give you another chance," her teacher continued. "You may turn in a proposal for another project by the end of the day on Monday. An original proposal, please."

Sylvia wanted to speak but couldn't get out any words. Her cheeks burned. She knew she should defend herself but instead left the classroom in shock. Racing to her locker, she pictured how sweetly Indra had asked her about her project in the lunchroom, and then stole it right from under her nose.

Now she understood the meaning of her mother's words. She should have trusted her gut.

Fighting back the sting of tears, Sylvia rushed out of the school and into the chilly autumn wind. The faster she walked, the harder she cried, until she found herself running. Falling into a steady rhythm, she became aware of the comforting beat of her feet on the pavement. As the fresh cool air filled her lungs, she began to feel better.

"Enough!" Sylvia shouted and came to a sudden stop. She thought about Eleanor Roosevelt's wise words and shouted, "They can't make me feel bad, unless I let them!"

Two girls passing by on bikes giggled at Sylvia talking loudly to herself. Taking a deep breath, she pushed back her shoulders and started walking again with deliberate steps. *I have to do what's right for me*, she thought. She didn't know exactly how, but she knew in her heart that she would find a way to come up with a new science experiment. Maybe even a better one.

16

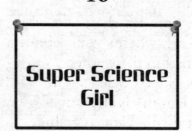

Super Science Girl

Mrs. Petersen read the sign on Sylvia's bedroom door. She tapped on the door and heard a muffled, "Who is it?" from within.

"It's your mother."

"Come on in, Mom."

Mrs. Petersen opened the door to see Sylvia in the middle of her bed with a laptop, surrounded by papers, books, and notebooks.

"Super Science Girl, I presume?" she asked with a smile.

"That's me, Mom."

"You have been in your bedroom a pretty long time for a Saturday morning. What are you up to?"

"I'm creating the world's best science experiment," Sylvia announced.

"What is it?"

"I don't quite know yet, but when I do, it will be the best."

"Well . . . I guess that's a good attitude." Her mom smiled. "Are you coming down for lunch?"

"No time for that."

"Make time for that, and while you are at it, Science Girl, where's your laundry? I'm going to throw a load in the washer."

"That's 'Super' Science Girl," Sylvia corrected. "And my laundry is all ready to go in the basket in my closet if you want to grab it."

Mrs. Petersen opened Sylvia's closet door, and as she lifted the basket full of dirty clothes, she spied something else. Reaching to the back corner of the closet floor, she picked up a couple of kitchen towels splattered with red stains.

"What are these?" she asked Sylvia, as she held up the towels by two fingers.

"Dish towels?" Sylvia responded cautiously.

Mrs. Petersen raised her left eyebrow and looked first at the towels and then at Sylvia.

"Dirty dish towels?" Sylvia stated, trying to soften her mother with a grin.

"Dish towels with red stains, to be more exact. Might these be my dish towels that you and Kristen mopped up your volcano mess with from over the summer?"

"You knew about the volcano?" Sylvia asked sheepishly.

"Science Girl or no Science Girl, you are going

to figure out how to clean these. Today!"

"Okay, Mom, I promise . . . as soon as I come up with a science experiment."

"You will take care of the towels now, young lady," Mrs. Petersen said as she opened her fingers to let the crumpled towels fall to the ground.

"All right."

Mrs. Petersen left the room and Sylvia stared at her computer screen. It was blank. She had been working on ideas all morning and had come up with nothing so far. *How could this be so hard?* she wondered. Crawling to the end of the bed, she reached to the floor to pick up the towels.

"Yuck," Sylvia said out loud. *How in the world am I going to get these clean?*

She turned back to her computer and typed in the search bar:

How to clean stains?

Like magic, the screen filled with half-a-dozen websites, each filled with ideas, including natural ways to clean things. Sylvia read about everything from using toothpaste and plant extracts to lemons and limes. *Funny,* she thought, *some are acidic and some are alkaline, the exact opposites.* She wondered which would work best and figured she could just try them and find out. As she scooped up the towels again, she stopped in her tracks.

"That's it! That's my science experiment! I'll

find out which natural products work best to clean stains."

Sylvia ran downstairs to the laundry area where her mother was working and gave her a big hug and kiss.

"You are brilliant, Mom!" Sylvia announced. "You solved my science experiment problem."

"I did?" Mrs. Petersen questioned, bewildered, as she watched Sylvia head to the refrigerator. *At least she's eating her lunch*, she thought. But when she saw Sylvia pass by with her arms cradling lemons, limes, soda water, baking powder, and vinegar, she knew her Super Science Girl was up to something again!

17

On Monday morning, Sylvia was in great spirits when she submitted the proposal for her new science experiment. Kristen and Indra walked into class together, and Kristen smiled at Sylvia. Sylvia looked at her without expression and pulled out her science book. She had decided that she was no longer going to get caught up with Kristen, Indra, and their drama.

"Sylvia," Kristen called out after class. "Wait up."

Sylvia turned and waited.

"I know you're mad that you couldn't be in our group," Kristen said. "But that doesn't mean you have to ignore me all together. I know I was pretty busy this summer with the wedding plans and all, and I'm sorry I missed your birthday. You shouldn't be mad at me just because I'm having fun with Indra and our friends. It's not like I've done anything wrong."

"You call stealing my science project idea not doing anything wrong?"

"What are you talking about?" Kristen's face showed surprise. "No one stole your science project."

"Indra did."

"That's not true. Indra is the one who came up with it."

"Really, you think she did?"

"Yes, and maybe if you would stop being so jealous, you wouldn't have to blame everything that goes wrong on her."

"Jealous! I'm not jealous. Honestly, I feel sorry for you, Kristen."

"Well, there's no need to be sorry for me because I'm perfectly happy. I have new friends, new clothes, and I'm popular for the first time in my life."

"Then it sounds like you have everything you ever wanted. But maybe if you would just open your eyes for a minute, you would see that Indra is just using you. Maybe you can't see what's happening because you have too much mascara on. She didn't come up with that experiment idea, I did!"

"Oh, my gosh, I can't believe you said that!" Kristen exclaimed. "And, I happen to like how I look, it makes me feel good. And I like having fun. Did you ever think of maybe wearing something other than those stupid T-shirts?"

"You used to like these 'stupid T-shirts.'" Sylvia stood straighter and put her hands on her hips with defiance.

"Yeah, well I used to like playing with dolls, too," Kristen snapped.

Both girls stopped talking and just stood face-to-face, staring, feeling the sting of each other's words.

"I'm sorry that Indra has you fooled, Kristen, but she doesn't have me fooled," Sylvia cautioned. "Just make sure you are doing what's right for you."

Sylvia turned on her heel and marched down the hall without looking back.

18

Over the next few weeks, Sylvia focused on her schoolwork and on completing her science project. Based on everything she researched, Sylvia prepared her hypothesis. She believed that lemons would do the best job for cleaning a variety of stains, and she busily set out to gather the data to prove it.

One day after school, she saw a girl pinning a poster to the bulletin board just outside of the school's main office. A drawing caught her eye because it looked similar to the robots she had seen at the robotics competition last summer. As she tried to see the rest of the poster, the girl turned to greet her.

"Hi, are you interested in the Robotics Club?" the girl asked.

Sylvia perked up her ears. "We have a Robotics Club at school?"

"It's our second year, and it's open to anyone in middle school. We start next week on Tuesday after school. Why don't you come and see what it's all about?"

Sylvia nodded. "I'd love that."

"Great! I'm Dede," the girl said. "I'm in eighth

grade. I recognize you from my honors science class, but you're in seventh grade, aren't you?"

"Yes," Sylvia replied. "I've seen you in class. Sorry I haven't said 'hi' before. I'm Sylvia. Thanks so much for inviting me to come to Robotics Club. I'll see you next week at the meeting."

"See you then! We meet in the gym," Dede said as she moved on to post another sign.

~~~

The following Tuesday, Sylvia arrived at the gym to find a group of about a dozen students talking excitedly as they huddled around a little robot. *It looks just like Robbie*, she thought. She smiled, remembering her day at the robotics competition last summer. She wanted to be part of the group, but she didn't see Dede and felt too shy to introduce herself. A few of the other students were from her science class, but they had never really talked to her before. Feeling like she didn't belong, Sylvia was about to leave when Dede entered the gym.

"Sylvia!" Dede called out. "You came!"

Sylvia looked at Dede's smiling face and suddenly felt happy and welcome.

"Let me introduce you to our team and to Simon."

"Who is Simon?" Sylvia asked.

"Our robot!" Dede laughed. "You know, when

we grow up, robots will be just about everywhere, and they will probably be able to do just about anything!"

"Really?" Sylvia was fascinated.

"Well, almost, anyway! Come on, I'll introduce you to the rest of our team," Dede offered.

Sylvia spent the next hour with the group of boys and girls who seemed as interested in her as she was in them. She knew very little about robotics, so was content to simply listen to what she could learn by being part of the club. She was excited that she would have a chance to help design, build, and program robots, and maybe someday be part of the competition team. The time flew by, and she recounted the afternoon in her mind on her walk home from school.

19

The next day, Dede and another girl Sylvia had met at Robotics Club spotted her in the lunchroom and asked her to join them. They talked the entire lunch period, and Sylvia told them about her trip to the robotics competition. She was pleased when they asked so many questions and seemed truly interested. One of the girls was on the school soccer team, and the other was practicing to perform in the school musical next semester. They seemed to like Sylvia for who she was, and that made her happy.

Kristen, on the other hand, rarely seemed to have a smile on her face these days. Each day, when she, Indra, Judy, and Nicole arrived at school, they showed off their new clothes and accessories. Sylvia had to admit Kristen looked great, but she looked like a puppy following Indra around, always agreeing with whatever she said. She thought they acted like the beehives she'd studied in fourth-grade science class, always swarming around Indra and treating her like the queen.

One day at lunch, Sylvia was seated with her friends from Robotics Club. A few of the students had brought in Rubik's® Cube three-dimensional puzzles. Each of them tried to solve the puzzle while one of the students used a stopwatch to see who was the fastest. A small crowd of students gathered around the table, and they erupted into cheers of encouragement each time someone solved the puzzle.

Just before it was Sylvia's turn, Indra showed up, curious to learn why someone else was the center of attention. Kristen, Judy, and Nicole followed close behind. To Sylvia's surprise, Kristen gave a thumbs-up to Sylvia, and Sylvia smiled back.

"Okay everyone, quiet!" Dede commanded as she held up a stopwatch and Sylvia prepared to start. A hush fell around the table.

"Geeks and freaks," Indra called out flatly. "Come on, girls." She motioned to Kristen, Judy, and Nicole. "This is for children."

Judy and Nicole followed quickly, and Kristen saw the hurt expression on Sylvia's face as a few of the kids who were watching left. Kristen mouthed the words *I'm sorry* but Sylvia looked away.

"Are you coming?" Kristen heard Indra calling her.

When they reached their table and sat down, Kristen didn't really feel like eating. She pushed her food around the tray with her fork as she thought about what had just happened. She didn't like how Indra had treated Sylvia or the other kids doing the puzzles.

"Indra, can I ask you something?" Kristen asked.

"Sure, what?"

"You know how you came up with our science project experiment?"

"Yes, don't you love it?" Indra smiled. "I think we are sure to win."

"Yeah, it's very good. But I was just wondering, how did you think of it?"

"What do you mean?" Indra looked at her innocently.

"I mean, what made you think of the idea?"

"You know, um, it just came to me."

"Just out of thin air?"

"Yep, just like that." Indra snapped her fingers and flashed a smile. "I really love the top you have on today. It makes your eyes look so pretty."

"Thanks," Kristen said, and looked away.

20

On Tuesday after school, Sylvia went to the gymnasium for Robotics Club and was surprised to see Kristen with a video camera, shooting some students playing basketball. She was able to see what Kristen was shooting on a monitor that was nearby.

"That was good," Sylvia said when Kristen stopped recording.

"Oh! You surprised me." Kristen turned around. "Thanks."

The girls stood in awkward silence for a moment as Kristen packed up the video camera the school had provided for the semester.

"You're getting very good," Sylvia said. "I saw the video you did of the fall carnival on the morning announcements."

"I really love doing it."

"It shows," Sylvia said. "You should do what you love to do. And I was wrong to tell you not to do it."

"That's okay."

The girls stood quietly, and Kristen nervously packed up her things.

"I'm here for the Robotics Club," Sylvia said.

"That's cool. I think you will be good at that."

"Well, I guess I better go join the group." Sylvia shrugged.

"Yeah, guess so, see you around."

When Sylvia got halfway across the gym floor, Kristen called out, "Hey, Sylvia!"

"Yeah?" Sylvia turned to see Kristen walking toward her.

"You know the science experiment that you said you thought of? How did you think it up?"

Sylvia explained how she was staring out the window when the colored lights of the church windows caught her eye and inspired her to think about how different-colored light would affect plant growth.

"Wow," was all Kristen could say, as it suddenly sunk in that Sylvia had been telling the truth the whole time. Everything Indra said had been a lie. And with the competition coming up in just a few days, it was too late to do anything about it.

"I'm so sorry," Kristen continued, "I just couldn't believe Indra would lie about something like that."

"Well, I wouldn't be surprised if she was lying to you about a whole lot more." Sylvia turned and joined her group on the other side of the gym, leaving Kristen standing in stunned silence.

21

The next morning, Indra was watching Max put the final touches on the group's experiment when Kristen met them in the science classroom to practice their presentation before class.

"Hi, Kristen," Indra said. She usually commented on Kristen's outfit, but today she took note of the plain T-shirt and blue jeans Kristen wore. She turned her attention back to Max.

"Hey." Kristen nodded to Indra and Max.

"What do you think?" Indra held up a big poster board that Max had created. "Isn't Max wonderful?" she gushed, smiling at Max, who turned red at the compliment. "I think we are going to win, don't you?"

"If we win, it will be because of a lie," Kristen said.

Indra stopped smiling. "What's that supposed to mean?"

"Indra, I know you stole our science experiment idea from Sylvia."

"I didn't steal it," Indra said in a defensive tone. "It's not like she owned it. Besides, she's the one who told me all about it. So actually she gave it to us."

"That's just not right," Kristen said firmly.

"Well, that's the way it is," Indra said and started coloring in a plant leaf on the poster. "And you will be happy when we get an A and win."

"Is that what all this is about?" Kristen asked. "Has our friendship just been about helping you get good grades?"

"Look, I'm getting what I need, and you are getting what you wanted."

"What do you mean by that?"

"If I don't get an A, I will never hear the end of it from my parents. That's all they care about." Indra furrowed her brow. "And do you remember what you looked like when we first met last summer? Pretty pathetic. Your friends, or should I say your only friend, was a loser. And now you dress right, think right, and are in the right group."

"Dress right? The right group? What's the 'right group'?"

"You're in my group," Indra announced proudly.

"Thanks for your concern, Indra, but I think I can figure out what to wear and what to say. And I certainly know what to think. And right now, I think you have it all wrong. I want friends who like me for who I am, not for what I wear. And I'm not going to think less of people because they think for themselves."

"Good luck with that. You just ended your

chance at being popular."

"No, Indra, I just ended our friendship."

22

Sylvia was sitting on her bed sorting through a pile of old T-shirts. She held one up and admired the sayings written on both sides, and then gave it a playful hug.

"Time to say good-bye to you." She dropped it into her wastebasket just as the doorbell rang. Sylvia could hear her mother's footsteps in the hallway as she headed to the door, followed by the sound of conversation.

"Sylvia!" her mother called out. "It's Kristen."

Sylvia sat up straight in surprise, paused for a moment, and finally called back, "She can come up!"

What could Kristen be doing here? She hadn't visited since the day Sylvia left for camp.

Kristen peeked her head around the door and asked quietly, "May I come in?"

"Sure," Sylvia replied cautiously.

Kristen walked in and started looking at some of the pictures on the bookshelf. There were photos of the girls together on the first day of kindergarten, and another one at science camp last year. She smiled as she thought of the years of fun she had shared with Sylvia.

Finally, turning to her friend, Kristen said with all her heart, "Sylvia, I am so sorry. You told me that Indra took your experiment idea, and I didn't listen to you. I was so wrong."

Sylvia thought for a moment. Then she said, "It's okay."

"No, it's not. I think in my heart I knew something was wrong. I just didn't want to believe it because I was having so much fun and felt so popular and had such cool friends. But it turns out they weren't cool and they weren't my friends at all. Indra was just using me and probably poor Max, too, to get a good grade in science. I don't even know what was real and what wasn't."

"I know."

Kristen sat down on the bed next to Sylvia and said, "I'm really sorry. I feel horrible about how I acted. And I feel stupid for trying to be someone I'm not. I can't tell you how much I've spent on clothes that I don't even like. And if I hear Judy or Nicole say 'definitely' one more time, I may gag."

"Oh my gosh, definitely!" Sylvia laughed, and then Kristen started laughing with her. The two fell back on the bed in a fit of giggles.

Kristen reached for a balled-up shirt that was under her head and held it up. "What are you doing with all your shirts here?" she asked.

"I'm getting rid of them. They're just silly."

"Who said they're silly?" Kristen asked.

"You, for one."

"I'm sorry, I did, didn't I?" Kristen felt ashamed. "These shirts aren't half as silly as some of the stuff I've been wearing these last two months."

"You can say that again!"

"Hey! You don't have to agree with me that quickly." Kristen laughed.

"How about I keep the T-shirts I love and you keep the clothes you love?"

"Deal!" Kristen said.

"Deal!" Sylvia nodded. Without thinking, both girls clapped their hands and performed their special handshake, just like old times.

Suddenly Kristen's eyes grew wide and she asked with concern, "So now that we've taken your experiment, what are you going to do?"

Sylvia got up and walked toward her desk as she explained, "Actually, I came up with a brilliant new experiment idea."

"Why doesn't that surprise me?"

"Remember the day we made that volcano?

"Tried to make a volcano." Kristen corrected her with a laugh. "That was a lot of fun."

"It was, but do you remember how we got red dye all over everything? Well . . . I sorta left those dirty things in a pile in the back of my closet, and my mom found them and made me try to clean them. I tried a bunch of ways to clean stains with stuff we had around the house. It turned out to be a great experiment to learn about acidity and alkaline solutions for cleaning."

Kristen listened intently and said, "It's good, Sylvia, really good!"

"Only one problem," Sylvia said. "I have to present it myself."

Kristen made a face. "I remember that presentation you did a couple of years ago about Marie Curie. Ouch."

"I'd like to forget that." Sylvia cringed.

"Aw, it wasn't that bad," Kristen said, trying to comfort her friend.

"Yes, it was."

"Yeah, it was pretty bad!" Kristen laughed, and Sylvia smiled as she clutched her own neck as though she was choking.

"I don't know what went wrong. I had the whole thing memorized."

"Maybe that was the problem. You just memorized it. Our video teacher taught us that a speaker who's passionate and knows her subject is much more interesting than someone who reads or memorizes a speech. It's all about telling a good story."

"That makes sense, but I memorized it because I was afraid."

"You're great when you talk to just me or your mom and dad. You know what you're talking about when it comes to science, and that makes me excited to listen!"

"I just get so nervous, and my face turns red in front of the class. I don't see how we can fix that by Friday. I don't care how good the experiment is. I don't think I can do it. I'll just turn in the written portion and take a C for the project."

"No, you can't do that!" Kristen exclaimed. "But to tell you the truth, I can't think of how we can get you ready by Friday." The girls sat quietly for a moment.

"Unless . . ." Kristen said slowly.

"Unless what?"

"Unless your best friend just had a brilliant idea!"

"Since when are you my best friend again?" Sylvia's voice was teasing.

"Since I just had a brilliant idea that is going to save your science presentation."

"Okay, so what is it?"

"No time for details," Kristen said as she headed for the door. "Just trust me, and bring everything you need for your presentation to the video lab tomorrow at 7:00 a.m. sharp!"

"Why so early?"

"Like I said, just trust me. I gotta get home for

dinner. Do you trust me?"

"Okay, I trust you." Sylvia nodded. "See you tomorrow."

"See you then," Kristen called out as she left the bedroom. Then she pointed to the sign on the door and added, "Super Science Girl!"

23

The next day, Sylvia walked briskly into the middle school building. She held a large box filled with the items she needed for her experiment: lemons, vinegar, salt, baking soda, and a variety of other food items, including a number of stained objects. It was just after seven o'clock and the lights were on in only a few of the classrooms, where teachers were preparing for the day ahead. The peaceful hallways were punctuated with the steady sound of her rubber soles squeaking on the clean floors. She was running late, so she passed her locker without stopping and went straight to the video room as Kristen had requested. Kristen was putting a battery in a video camera.

"I'm here!" Sylvia announced.

"Good morning, Super Science Girl!" Kristen yelled with enthusiasm.

Sylvia rolled her eyes and asked, "So what is all this about?"

"Well," Kristen began. "You have a terrific experiment, right?"

"Yes."

"And you have to present it to a group, but you're afraid, right?"

"Unfortunately, yes. What's your point?"

"I'm going to videotape your presentation."

"You're going to what?" Sylvia furrowed her eyebrows, puzzled. "Why would you videotape me?"

"Because you can tell me all about your experiment just like you always do, and it will be great. Then, when it's your turn to present, we'll show your videotape as part of your presentation!"

Sylvia said nothing as she absorbed what Kristen had said.

"I don't know. I'm not sure this is a good idea."

"Of course it's a good idea. What's wrong with it?"

"I don't know, but I'm sure something is wrong with it."

"Like what?"

"I don't know."

"There's nothing wrong with it! Are you in?"

Sylvia took a deep breath, trying to think of a reason not to move forward with the idea, and finally said, "I'm in!"

"Excellent!" Kristen announced. "Let's get started. You spread out everything you need on the table. First you'll introduce yourself; then you can state your hypothesis, and then point out all the items you need for your experiment.

"I've brought a few props for you to use,"

Kristen continued, as she pulled a long item out of a box. It looked like a stick with a large orange arrow at the end.

"What in the world is that?" Sylvia asked.

"It's a pointer!" Kristen said, looking very pleased with herself as she pointed at a variety of things with the crazy arrow. "After you show what you need, you can describe the experiment, explain the outcome, and come to a conclusion. Then this evening, I'll edit all the video footage and put it together. It will be great!"

Sylvia was getting nervous about the idea, but there was no time to change her mind. Her presentation was tomorrow. She knew if she didn't try this, she would have to do the presentation anyway. "Okay."

"Are you ready?"

"Ready."

"Sylvia, the Super Science Girl, take one," Kristen directed as she pressed the record button, pointed to Sylvia, and called out, "Action!"

Sylvia stared at the camera for a few seconds, let out a big breath, and said, "Wait, I'm not sure how to act."

"Just act like yourself," Kristen said as she peered through the viewfinder.

"I can't act like myself. I'm boring," Sylvia said.

"No, you're not," Kristen assured her. "I like

you best when you act like yourself."

"I thought you liked how your new friends acted."

Kristen stopped recording and put the camera down so she could look at her friend. "That's exactly what was wrong with them," Kristen began. "They were acting. It wasn't real. And it turned out they weren't my real friends. You are real, though, and that's what's so great about you."

"Really?" Sylvia waved the orange pointer in the air and struck a pose.

"Really." Kristen smiled. "Just act like you do when we're goofing around doing experiments, and it will be fine."

"I can't believe I'm doing this!" Sylvia said.

"Ready?" Kristen asked.

"Ready."

"Here goes nothin'!" Kristen called out as she pressed the record button. "Action!"

24

"You might want to chew that first," Mr. Petersen said to Sylvia.

Sylvia was shoveling food into her mouth. She was having trouble containing her excitement about the science competition.

"Tomorrow is your big day," Mrs. Petersen noted. "You haven't said a thing about your science experiment. Are you ready?"

"I'm ready," Sylvia said as she scooped a fork full of mashed potatoes into her mouth.

"Your dad and I are coming in to see the presentations. Do you need any help practicing?" Mrs. Petersen asked.

"That's okay, Mom, I've got it."

"That's good, honey," her mother said with a mix of surprise and concern. Usually Sylvia was so nervous before a presentation that she wouldn't be able to eat. "Are you sure you don't need any help?"

"Really, Mom, I'm not nervous. And don't worry, I didn't try to memorize it again. May I have another piece of chicken, please?"

"Your dad and I are happy to help you practice if you want, dear." Mrs. Petersen passed the serving dish to Sylvia. She shot a worried look to her husband, who shrugged. "There's nothing to be ashamed of if you need some help," she continued. "I know how hard it is for you to talk in front of a group."

"Thanks, Mom, but really, I've got everything under control."

Mrs. Petersen tried to curb her need to protect Sylvia and smoothed the tablecloth instead. Something was definitely going on, but she guessed she and Mr. Petersen would just have to wait for the competition to see for themselves.

25

The gymnasium was buzzing with activity when Sylvia arrived at school the next morning. She ran straight across the wooden floor to read a poster set up on an easel that listed the thirteen teams from two classes that would present today. Sylvia hoped she would be scheduled early so she could get it over with. As she skimmed the list, she didn't see her name, until she reached the bottom, where it finally appeared. Last. She felt her spirits sink and started worrying if the video idea would work after all.

"Having second thoughts?" Kristen asked, startling her.

"I'm last," Sylvia exclaimed, relieved to see her friend.

"That's okay."

"No, it's not. Everyone will be here at the end, all the kids, all the teachers, all the parents."

"It'll be fine," Kristen said, as she handed over a disc with Sylvia's presentation on it. "Good luck, you'll be great!"

Indra and Max walked toward the girls. Glancing at the list, they saw that their team would present fourth. Indra flashed a big smile and said, "Hi girls, all ready for the big day?"

"Hi, Indra, hi Max," Kristen said.

Sylvia could contain herself no longer. Taking a deep breath, she said, "Indra, what you did was wrong. You used my science experiment and you used my friend."

Indra's mouth dropped open in surprise.

"I don't know where you get these ideas," she answered sweetly. "Besides, after today, it won't matter. We'll win the science competition, and get As. You will probably get an A in science with or without your silly experiment. I needed it more than you. So what's the big deal? Everyone wins."

"Is that all that matters to you, getting an A?" Sylvia was incredulous.

"Did I hear someone say that my Indra is getting an A?" Indra's mother surprised them as they turned to see Mr. and Mrs. Patel, who had just arrived. It was hard not to notice Mrs. Patel, who wore a cream wool jacket with black trim over a black silk shirt and a matching skirt. She held a designer handbag with her beautifully manicured hand.

"We are so proud of our Indra," Mrs. Patel continued. "She is just like her big sister, all As since she started school. And if she continues to be like her sister, she will be the number-one student in her class. You know, Indra's sister won the science competition at her school years ago, and we expect Indra to bring home the winning trophy this year. Don't disappoint us, sweetheart." Her mother smiled and left with Mr. Patel to find seats near the front.

The color drained from Indra's face, and suddenly she didn't seem so tough. Sylvia thought she looked like she was going to cry. The four of them stared at each other in silence. The sound of someone tapping a microphone, followed by the booming voice of Mrs. Carter, caught their attention. "Welcome to the 14th annual science competition!"

"Come on, let's go get ready to present," Indra barked to Kristen and Max. She wiped her eye with her sleeve and turned to go. "Let's win this thing."

26

Sylvia saw her parents sitting in the third row. As much as she was happy they were supporting her, she worried about whether they would like the video idea. She took a seat with a few of the other students on the gymnasium floor to watch the presentations. When Kristen's turn came, she moved a little closer to the center so she could have a better view.

Indra opened the presentation with her dazzling smile. Then Kristen explained the experiment and the data they had collected about how the different-colored lights affected plant growth. She used notecards and spoke with such ease and confidence as she went on to introduce the group's hypothesis. They had amazing charts and posters that Max had skillfully created. It was a wonderful experiment, and the presentation was perfect. Sylvia thought it was everything she had imagined her experiment would be, and it broke her heart that her idea had been stolen.

When the group completed their presentation, the applause was long and loud. Mrs. Patel jumped to her feet and clapped with enthusiasm. She leaned to the woman to her right and said, "That's my daughter." Indra basked in the attention, and Sylvia felt even worse. With growing dread, she sat through the next eight presentations until the teacher finally announced, "Next we will hear from Sylvia Petersen, who will present her hypothesis about natural ways to clean stains."

Her heart pounding rapidly, Sylvia walked to the front and up two steps to a platform, which had been specially erected for the competition. She organized a few items on a table. From the opposite side of the steps, Kristen wheeled over a large video screen on a cart, and Sylvia inserted the disc. She could see a look of disbelief on Indra's face as Kristen nodded that it was okay to begin.

"Hi, everyone," Sylvia said. Scanning the crowd, she realized it had grown. Not only were all of the student participants and their family members there, other teachers and classmates had assembled. There was even a reporter from a local newspaper and a TV crew. The familiar fear swept over her, and she could feel the color draining from her face. Sylvia saw her mother smiling, but it did not mask her worried look. An awkward silence filled the air as people shifted in their seats and someone coughed. Sylvia looked at Kristen, who was making a funny face at her. It reminded her of Kristen's words, *just be yourself.*

"I love science," Sylvia suddenly blurted out.

"Exploring, experimenting, and discovering things is amazing, and it's the reason we have rockets going to space and technology that keeps us connected wherever we are. It's even the reason we have long-lasting lipstick." The audience laughed. "So that's why this competition is so great. It helps us learn how to follow our curiosity and to learn about the world around us." Sylvia looked directly at Indra. "And science means everything to me. I know for some of us it's just a class we have to get through. It's just another grade. But science is what I want to do. Today really isn't about getting a grade or winning or losing, it's about the experience. It's about working and learning together and making a real difference."

Indra looked at her feet, ashamed.

"Sorry about all that," Sylvia continued. "I just thought that was important to say because sometimes I don't speak up. I'm not very good at talking in front of a group, and I think my parents can confirm that. In fact, right now, I would guess that my mom is pretty sure I'm going to get ill, because that's what typically happens. So, my best friend decided to help me solve that problem. For my science experiment, I explored which natural substances would make the best stain removers. And, of course, to remove stains, you first have to make stains. Mom, please know that your dish towel was sacrificed in the name of science. And now, may I present, 'Sylvia's Super Science Girl Show!'"

Sylvia nodded to Kristen, who pressed the button on the DVD player.

"Hi! It's Sylvia, the Super Science Girl, with an awesome experiment that will come in handy if you just happen to explode an ink pen on your shirt, spill ketchup on the carpet, or chocolate on the sofa. You can either hide the stain or blame it on the dog, or you can discover how to get rid of stains with stuff you probably already have hanging around the house!"

The audience turned their attention to the video, watching and listening with interest as Sylvia described her experiment on the screen. Six minutes later the video ended. Sylvia finished her presentation by saying, "And that's how I proved my hypothesis: that lemon juice and vinegar are great natural stain removers. Thank you!"

For a moment, the entire gymnasium was silent. Sylvia wished she was invisible and turned awkwardly to leave the platform. To her surprise, applause washed over the audience like a wave, and within seconds everyone was on their feet giving a standing ovation. Shocked, Sylvia broke into a wide grin and turned back to face the audience. She spotted Kristen, who gave her two thumbs-up. Sylvia's parents were clapping, smiling, and waving.

Mrs. Carter walked to the microphone and announced, "Thank you, Sylvia, for a thoughtful experiment and a very creative presentation. We will now take a ten-minute break to score the presentations and announce the top three winners. Will all students report to the front of the gymnasium, please?"

The gym was abuzz with conversation as Indra wound her way through the crowd to Kristen, with Nicole and Judy following closely behind.

"So! I thought we had this won until I saw the little show your friend just put on. Is it true that you helped her with that video? That's what people are saying."

"Yes, and I'm proud of it, especially after you took her experiment. Besides, winning isn't everything, Indra."

"You're right, winning isn't everything, it's the only thing," Indra said slyly. "And trust me, I will win."

Just then Sylvia appeared, smiling and flushed. She and Kristen did their special handshake and laughed with delight.

"What was that supposed to be?" Indra questioned as she observed the handshake in disbelief.

"Oh, my gosh!" Nicole interrupted as she congratulated Sylvia. "Your presentation was awesome!" Nicole gushed.

"Awesome!" Judy chimed in.

"Shut up, Judy," Indra snapped so loudly that a group of kids nearby turned to look.

Shocked, Judy stopped in mid-sentence.

"Excuse me, Kristen, but I think I asked you a question," Indra demanded. "I repeat, what was that supposed to be?" She waved her hands in the air with exaggeration to mimic the girls' handshake.

All eyes turned to Kristen.

"It's our special handshake." Kristen emphasized each word. She looked around the crowd that had gathered, took a breath, and then announced, "We started it in Girl Scouts together."

"Girl Scouts?" asked Indra in disbelief.

"Yes, Girl Scouts." Kristen's voice conveyed her confidence. "I'm a Girl Scout and I'm proud of it. In fact, I love it."

"Oh. My. Gosh!" Indra exclaimed. "How lame." She looked at Judy and Nicole for approval, but the girls looked away.

Sylvia's eyes grew wide, and for a tense moment no one said a thing, wondering what would happen next.

Max, who was watching the exchange, finally

said, "I don't see what's so lame about Girl Scouts. I'm a Boy Scout."

"I'm a Girl Scout," said another girl who was looking on.

"So am I," said an eighth-grade student.

"Fine," Indra responded. "So you are all losers."

"No, Indra, it's not fine," Kristen responded. "None of this has been fine. The truth is that you took advantage of Sylvia to get an idea for our experiment. And what's worse is that I went along with everything just so I could be your friend. I tried doing all the things you thought were cool and stopped doing things I loved. You were just using me, just like you are using Max, Judy, and Nicole."

Judy and Nicole looked at each other and exchanged frowns.

"A real friend doesn't have to dress or think like you do, or do all the same things you do," Kristen continued.

Judy looked down at her outfit and realized she was dressed similarly to Nicole and Indra.

"You're right," Judy said. "No one should be judged just by how she looks."

Nicole was shocked that Judy would stand up to Indra. Then she nodded her head in agreement.

Kristen continued, "Sylvia is one of the smartest and nicest girls in school, and she works hard and is so much fun. She's honest, and that's why she's such a good friend. And you owe her an apology!"

"The only thing I'm sorry about is that I wasted time with you, Kristen!" Indra turned to Sylvia. "Don't think that little video trick you pulled with your experiment is going to keep us from winning. I don't care if it was the best presentation; my mom is taking care of that right now."

The girls looked toward the judges to witness Mrs. Patel speaking to them and pointing her finger directly in the face of Mrs. Carter, whose brow was furrowed.

"You can't do that!" Kristen exclaimed.

"I can and I just did." Indra looked pleased with herself. "I told my mom that you broke the rules, Sylvia. Looks like you are going to be disqualified. Sorry, but like my mom says, everybody loves a winner. That's why I've got the grades, the looks, and the friends."

"I don't think so," Judy said meekly.

"You don't think what?" Indra demanded.

"I don't think you've got the friends, at least not me." Judy turned to leave. She patted Sylvia's shoulder and said, "Great job, Sylvia."

"Me, neither," Nicole said, following Judy.

"Thanks," Sylvia said to both girls.

The microphone made a noisy screech when it clicked on, "Let's all quiet down and be seated as we announce the winners of this year's science competition," Mrs. Carter said.

Sylvia was on pins and needles, wondering if she truly had been disqualified.

"Please join me in congratulating Dede Bauer, Jack Boyarsky, and Lin Choi, our third-place team, who investigated how the pH of different beverages affects our digestive systems. Please come to the podium to receive your ribbons and have your photo taken."

The excited team jumped up with enthusiasm, and the audience applauded as they gathered for a photo with Mrs. Carter and the principal.

"In second place, we applaud Sylvia Petersen for her experiment to discover the best natural stain removers." A murmur of surprise spread through the audience. On the one hand, Sylvia was thrilled that she had not been disqualified. But on the other, her hopes of winning had been dashed.

Mrs. Carter quickly continued, "While we all applaud Sylvia for her innovative video, as one of our concerned parents pointed out, the presentations have always been made in person, so points were deducted from her score; however, her creativity is to be commended. Please come up to receive your second-place medal, Syliva"

Kristen called out, "Way to go, Sylvia!" and

clapped as hard as she could. The rest of the audience joined in and rose to their feet. Sylvia felt all eyes on her as she walked toward the platform. She realized that even if she hadn't come in first, she had done the best job she could, and she had her best friend back! Her smile stretched from ear to ear for her photo as Mrs. Carter placed a medal hanging from a ribbon around her neck.

Sylvia's teacher shook her hand, pulled her a little closer, and gave her a hug as she whispered, "I pride myself on being a good judge of character, but I think I was wrong about you, Sylvia. I'm sorry that I doubted you, and I should have listened better."

"That's okay, Mrs. Carter." Sylvia smiled. "I know what you mean. Sometimes you just have to trust your gut!"

Mrs. Carter turned back to the microphone and said, "And in first place, please join me in congratulating the team of Indra Patel, Kristen Dawson, and Max Munts, who tested how different-colored lights affect plant growth."

Mrs. Carter looked directly at Sylvia and smiled as she announced to the audience, "It was an exceptional idea. Please come up to receive your first-place trophies." The audience applauded from their seats and, noticeably, Mr. and Mrs. Patel stood up to cheer for their daughter.

When the event was over, the children made their way to their families, who had lined up at tables of refreshments. The girls saw Mrs. Patel seeking out the news reporter. Kristen and Sylvia rolled their eyes.

"There she goes again," Kristen said.

The two joined their mothers, who were enjoying cups of iced tea together.

"We are so proud of you girls." Mrs. Petersen praised them both and hugged her daughter.

"Thanks, Mom," Sylvia said.

"Thanks, Mrs. Petersen," Kristen replied.

Then Sylvia saw Indra and her mother headed their way, with the reporter in tow.

"This is Mr. Reilly from Channel 10," Indra announced with importance. "He wants to interview us." Indra looked smugly at Sylvia as she emphasized, "It looks like the winners are going to be on TV."

"Oh, I'm sorry if you misunderstood," the reporter said, interrupting her. "Actually, I was asking if I could speak to the young lady who did the video presentation." He smiled at Sylvia and extended his hand to introduce himself to her.

Indra's face twisted into a look of shock and dismay. "What?" she cried. "Why? She didn't win, we did."

The reporter ignored Indra. "I have to hand

115

it to you, that was one of the best presentations I've ever seen from someone your age," he said. "In fact, maybe any age." He laughed as Sylvia's parents beamed.

"You really have a great way of making science understandable and explaining things with enthusiasm!" the reporter continued. "You may not have won, but I think you did a great job."

"Thanks!" Sylvia smiled. "I have to admit, I really wanted to win. But somehow I don't think that if I'd won I could be happier than I am right now. I heard someone say winning is the only thing, but I guess it's not!"

Indra stiffened and looked down at her feet as she thought about how she had treated Sylvia. Everything she was taught to do was always about winning and being the best. Her mother scolded her. "That should have been you talking to the reporter! Let's go. I'll hold your trophy for you. This will look perfect on the mantel next to your sister's."

The girls saw that Indra's eyes were full of tears when she turned to leave.

27

Later that evening, Sylvia, who was still wearing her medal, was finishing a celebration dinner with her parents when the doorbell rang. She jumped up from her chair and called out, "I'll get it." She ran to answer the door in stocking feet. About five feet from the screen door, she turned her body sideways to slide the rest of the way.

"Hi!" Sylvia greeted Kristen, who was standing on the doorstep holding a helium balloon with CONGRATULATIONS! printed on it.

"Are you ready for your TV debut?" she asked as she handed the balloon to Sylvia.

"I'm so excited," Sylvia replied. "Come on in, it starts in a few minutes!"

Kristen and Sylvia and her family assembled in front of the television in the living room. Mrs. Petersen came in with a bowl of popcorn and reminded Mr. Petersen to record the show. They sat through twenty minutes of news, and Sylvia wondered whether her interview was even going to be on.

"After the break, we reveal the winners of the annual Haverford Middle School Science Competition, and we'll talk to a local middle school student who is making science fun," the announcer said. The girls squealed with delight. When the commercial break was over, Mr. Reilly, the reporter they had met earlier, was on the screen.

REPORTER: At the annual science fair competition at Haverford Middle School today, students competed with a variety of clever concepts. Even though Sylvia Petersen didn't take home the first-place trophy, she captivated the audience with an original video show that made science not only more understandable, but fun! She calls it 'Sylvia's Super Science Girl Show!' Sylvia, how did you come up with your show idea?

SYLVIA: It was really my best friend, Kristen, who helped me do the presentation on video. I've always had trouble speaking in front of a big group, so she said I should just be myself and that she would record it. So that's what we did!

The girls smiled as they watched the news broadcast.

"Look, there you are on stage, Sylvia!" Kristen pointed to the TV. More video showed Kristen's team and Dede's team receiving their awards, as the reporter announced their names.

REPORTER: *What advice do you have for coming up with a good idea for an experiment?*

SYLVIA: *At first, I thought it was so hard to come up with ideas, but then I realized that science ideas are all around us. All you have to do is be curious about how things work, how they could work better, faster, maybe stronger, and then come up with a way to test your ideas.*

REPORTER: *So Sylvia, do you intend to make any more science videos?*

SYLVIA: *Yes, I do. In fact, Kristen and I are planning to have a weekly website show. It will not only show how to do the experiments but we are also going to use science principles to make cool things— like telescopes, rockets, and volcanoes!*

"What!" Kristen shrieked in shock. "We are?"
"Wait, it gets better," Sylvia advised.

REPORTER: *Would you consider letting us show your upcoming videos on the News10 website? We could call the series* Sylvia's Science Girl Show. *What do you think?*

SYLVIA: *I'd love that! But I was thinking that*

maybe you could call it Sylvia's SUPER Science Girl Show!

REPORTER: You've got a deal, young lady! Stay tuned next for sports and weather.

The newscast cut to a commercial break, and Kristen shrieked with delight. "You were amazing. Are we really going to do the science show?"

"Absolutely!"

Mr. Petersen turned to Sylvia and said, "Way to go, Einstein!"

"Thank you, Mr. Edison," Sylvia replied, naming another famous scientist.

28

"That was exciting to see your school on the news, wasn't it?" Mrs. Patel said as she clicked the remote to turn off the TV.

"I guess so," Indra agreed half-heartedly. But the truth was that she felt awful.

"Don't be blue. I know you are disappointed that they featured the other girl on TV instead of you, but you can be proud that you won. Your presentation was flawless and your experiment was excellent. I wouldn't be surprised if your teacher gives you extra credit."

The more her mother praised her, the worse Indra felt. Somehow this wasn't how she expected to feel after winning. Mostly she was thinking about the look on Sylvia's face and the sting of her words: *What you did was wrong. You used my science experiment and you used my friend.*

"I know I should be happy, but I don't feel that good about it," Indra confessed.

"What do you mean?"

Indra couldn't bear to admit what she had done and stumbled for the right words. "I didn't exactly think up the science experiment myself."

"Oh, is that what's bothering you?" Mrs. Patel

asked. "It was a team effort. As long as you don't take all the credit for yourself, it's fine. I'm so very proud of you. But I have to admit I, too, was a little disappointed that the reporter didn't spotlight the winners."

"No, Mom, you don't understand, Sylvia should have won."

"Indra, even if she had followed the rules and presented correctly, your experiment was better. Rest assured, the best experiment won."

"That's what I'm trying to tell you . . . the best experiment did win, but it wasn't my idea, it was Sylvia's."

"Explain what you mean, Indra." Mrs. Patel's brow began to furrow.

Indra launched into a detailed account of her conversation at the lunch table, where Sylvia explained her idea to her and how Indra then shared it with her teammates.

"My team was so impressed, I couldn't tell them it wasn't my idea, and besides Sylvia shared it with me. We did all the work. And like you say, you have to do everything you can to succeed. Everyone loves a winner. Isn't that right, Mom?" As the words tumbled out, she started to feel a little better and was sure her mother would see her point. But, judging from her mother's raised eyebrows, she began to have doubts.

"Are you going to say anything, Mom?"

"I'm not sure where to even begin," Mrs. Patel said gravely. "First of all, let's get something straight. When I tell you to do anything necessary to succeed, I mean study. Work harder. Go above and beyond. And when I say everyone loves a winner, I mean there is great satisfaction with a job well done. What you did was selfish and hurtful. I know at times I can be pushy, but it's because I want the best for my daughters. But not at any cost."

For the next ten minutes, Indra received the lesson of a lifetime.

"Now what am I going to do, Mom?"

"You are going to have to make this right, young lady."

"How do I do that?"

"You have all weekend to think about that." As she left to go into the kitchen, Mrs. Patel turned back and added, "Especially since you are grounded for the rest of it."

~ ~ ~

By Sunday afternoon, Indra had hatched a plan to make things right. She would go into school early and meet with Mrs. Carter before class to explain what had happened and apologize for her actions. Then she would apologize to Sylvia and her team. She knew she would take a lot of heat for it, but at least she would set the record straight. And this way she could patch things up quietly without everyone in the class knowing what she had done.

29

At school on Monday, Sylvia decided that this must be how a rock star feels. From the moment she walked through the double doors, her classmates were congratulating her with pats on the shoulder and words of praise.

"Hey, Sylvia, I saw you on the news, way to go!"

"Great video. I saw it on the Channel 10 website. It was cool!"

"Are you really going to have a science show? That's awesome!"

When she arrived at science class, Kristen had saved her a seat. Indra avoided looking at them as she paced back and forth near Mrs. Carter's desk waiting for her to arrive. She had been waiting for twenty minutes, but there was no sign of her teacher.

Finally, Mrs. Carter appeared, deep in conversation with Ms. Fischer, the principal.

"Excuse me, Mrs. Carter, may I speak to you?" Indra interrupted politely.

"Good morning, Indra," Mrs. Carter said cheerfully. "Congratulations on your excellent work."

"Thank you. May I speak to you, please?"

"In a moment. I'm speaking to Ms. Fischer."

Indra thought they would never stop talking when Mrs. Carter finally turned to her and asked her what she wanted.

"I wanted to tell you that I . . ."

Bing Bong Bing . . . the chiming sound of notes from a xylophone blared through the loudspeaker to mark the beginning of the morning announcements.

No! Indra thought. *Not now!*

"Indra, why don't you have a seat, and we can chat after class," Mrs. Carter suggested.

"But it will only take a minute . . . ."

"Please be seated, Indra."

Indra felt a wave of panic come over her, and she slumped in her seat as the color drained from her face.

When the announcements ended, Mrs. Carter greeted the class, "Good morning, I hope you all had a good weekend after all of the excitement surrounding the science fair competition. First, please join me in congratulating Sylvia. You represented our school, and especially the science department, beautifully on TV."

Sylvia smiled as her classmates applauded.

"Next, I would like to bring up the winners of the science fair to tell us about the inspiration for their experiment. Max, Indra, and Kristen, please come up to the front."

Indra's worst fears were coming true as the three made their way to the front of the room and faced the class.

"As we all know, sometimes the most difficult thing in science is to determine what you want to research," Mrs. Carter said. "And I was very impressed with the team's idea to explore whether different-colored lights affected the growth of plants differently. Let's learn about their inspiration for . . ."

"Excuse me, Mrs. Carter," Indra interrupted.

"Yes?" Mrs. Carter acknowledged Indra.

"Um, I just wanted, I mean, there's something I wanted to say."

The classroom fell silent and every eye was fixed on her. Indra stood motionless. Her mind felt mixed up, and she wasn't sure what she was going to say or do next. She took a big breath and continued.

"I just thought I should set something straight."

"Go on." Mrs. Carter gave her a nod of encouragement.

"Our experiment idea wasn't exactly original. It was actually Sylvia's idea."

Gasps could be heard from her classmates, and Max and Kristen watched in amazement as Indra confessed.

Indra continued speaking slowly and deliberately. "Max and Kristen didn't know anything about it. I told them it was my idea. I now know what I did was really wrong. It was stupid, and I just wanted to say I'm sorry to Max and Kristen, and I'm really sorry, Sylvia. I was wrong."

Tears streamed down Indra's face as she hurried to her desk to pick up a bag and placed it on Sylvia's desk. "This is for you, Sylvia."

Sylvia reached in and pulled out Indra's trophy. Indra turned and ran out the door, the sound of her shoes echoing down the empty hall. Mrs. Carter excused herself and followed Indra down the hallway and into the girls' restroom. Kristen and Sylvia followed. They stayed out of sight but watched the exchange between their teacher and Indra.

Mrs. Carter handed a tissue to Indra and spoke in a calm voice, "You know what you did was very wrong, Indra."

"I know, Mrs. Carter. I'm so ashamed."

"What you did was also brave," Mrs. Carter continued. "It takes a lot to admit you've done something wrong. It's especially hard to apologize in public, but I'm glad you did the right thing. Why did you steal Sylvia's idea?"

"I wanted to win and get an A. I wanted people to like me. I figured if I won the fair, it would solve everything."

"And did it?"

"No, it made everything worse. I felt so bad over the weekend that I told my mom what happened. I thought she would stick up for me because she's always telling me how important it is to get good grades. But when she found out what happened, I got into even more trouble. She said, 'It's not about the grades, it's about the journey,' and without putting in the hard work, I wouldn't learn anything. All this time, I thought it was just about the grades. I thought that's what my parents wanted. I think I blamed everything on them because it was hard for me to make friends when I switched schools. What's worse is that I still don't understand science! And, I used my friends. I know they probably hate me now. They only liked me because I had nice stuff. No one ever liked me for who I was."

"Maybe they never got to know the real Indra," Mrs. Carter suggested.

"I guess you're probably right," Indra admitted. "I've been pretending to be cool ever since I came to this school."

Just then, Sylvia and Kristen timidly poked their heads out from around the edge of the wall.

"Sorry that we followed you, Mrs. Carter, but it was because we were worried about Indra. And, we don't hate you, Indra."

"You should."

"Yeah, we probably should." Kristen smiled, and Indra tried to smile back, wiping away her tears.

"You realize, Indra, that you won't be getting an A for your work, don't you?" Mrs. Carter asked.

"Yes, I understand."

"And you are going to have to work hard to bring your grade back up," she continued.

"Yes."

"Anything else before we get back to class?" Mrs. Carter asked.

"Yes, just one more thing. What I don't understand is that even after I won, I didn't feel happy about it. But Sylvia, you were happy even though you didn't win. And you got all the attention."

Sylvia shrugged and said, "I guess scientists don't do all that research just to win a prize. They do it because they want to discover things. I loved doing the experiment, and I was just happy I had done my best."

"Sylvia's excellence was recognized in other ways beyond a prize," Mrs. Carter observed. "I think that's true whether you are talking about playing a sport, practicing a musical instrument, or working on an art project or a science assignment. There are many ways to define winning."

"Sylvia," Indra said, "you really deserved that trophy. I'm so sorry for what I did."

"Apology accepted," Sylvia replied.

"You are about the most normal person I've ever met, no matter what anyone says."

All the girls laughed and Indra continued, "What I mean to say is that you go after what you want, and people like you for who you are. I wish I could be more like that."

"And Kristen, I really messed up," Indra said. "I'm sorry that I tried to use you to help me win the science fair. I didn't really add much to the team. And you never needed to buy all those clothes to be my friend. I thought people were my friends only because I had cool things. I felt like I always had to take them to our club for them to like me. I know you weren't like that."

"You're right, I'm not," Kristen said. "But I have to admit, I probably would never have taken that video class if you hadn't told me about it. And I love it."

"More like bullied you into it." Indra cringed.

"Yeah, we might have to work on your approach a little."

Their teacher looked at her watch. "Now,

speaking of class, I have a class to teach. Let's get back to work."

The girls walked quickly out to the hall. Mrs. Carter followed them and watched the girls chatter as they headed back to class together.

"We didn't know you were so worried about pleasing your parents and fitting in at school," Sylvia said. "It always seemed like you had everything under control."

"Guess I had everyone fooled for a while, including myself."

"You still have a lot going for you," Sylvia said. "And, besides, you have at least two friends, that is, if you want us."

"Really?" Indra asked.

Kristen nodded.

"Thanks." She broke into a wide smile. "I'd really like that."

"And if you want, we can tutor you on weekends in science," Sylvia offered.

"Really? I would really like that."

"Really!" both girls blurted out in unison and started to laugh.

"I say that too much, don't I?" Indra looked at them sheepishly.

"Maybe just a little." Kristen smiled.

"Definitely," Sylvia added.

The girls all laughed and Indra continued, "I

would love if you would tutor me."

"We can start this weekend," Kristen suggested.

"That would be great. I'm free all this weekend."

"Actually, in that case, you can come to Girl Scouts Discover Day with us," Sylvia announced. It's this Saturday!"

"Uh oh, what's that?" Indra wrinkled her brow.

"We're going to learn how chemistry is used to make stuff."

"Like what?"

"Like a whole bunch of different kinds of formulas," Sylvia explained.

"Oh," Indra said flatly. "I don't know . . . ."

"Including formulas for lip gloss," Kristen added.

"Lip gloss, really?" Indra's eyes lit up. "I didn't know lip gloss has something to do with science."

"Of course it does, silly," Sylvia confirmed. Everything has something to do with science!"

THE END

Meet Sylvia Todd:

The inspiration behind "Sylvia Petersen"

The inspiration for the Sylvia character is Sylvia Todd, who became an Internet sensation at age eight when she created her own web show, *Sylvia's Super-Awesome Maker Show*. Since then, she has shown her science projects at the White House, written her own science book, and been profiled in the *New York Times* and *People* magazine.

"I've always been interested in making and doing things hands-on," says Sylvia. "I think the best way to ignite kids' imaginations is through making things."

Sylvia's passion for making things began with her father, who enjoyed building and creating things when he was young. One day, when Sylvia was five years old, he took her to a Maker Faire, where people who design things for fun gather to show off their creations. Sylvia was hooked, and she decided to make her first project: a solar-powered robotic car.

"It was fun and scary and frustrating–but I made something," she says. "By failing and pushing through the hard parts, I learned a whole lot. So really, it wasn't a failure at all."

Soon Sylvia and her father decided to make their

own Web show, where they created electronic projects and taught other kids how to do it, too. *Sylvia's Super-Awesome Maker Show* has enjoyed millions of views online. Sylvia creates everything from circuit boards and rocket ships to an LED shield and lava lamps.

"Making real things out of junk is what I love," she says. "Overcoming your own problems only to create something so real and personal in the end, however small, feels huge and wonderful."

At age twelve, Sylvia became an author by launching a series of full-color children's books, *Sylvia's Super-Awesome Project Books.* She enjoys being a Girl Scout and is the eldest of four children. She wants to be an astronaut or aeronautical engineer when she grows up. Until then, she continues to encourage other kids to learn through making.

Her biggest piece of advice to other kids is what she's been saying for years on her Web show:

"Get out there and make something!"

GIRLS WANT TO KNOW...

ASKED PATRICIA WOODY:
(the engineer who was the inspiration behind the Patricia Woods character)

WHAT IS A MAKER? A maker is someone who creates things. It can be anything, and I believe most girls would be surprised to find out how many things they create that they never associate with being a science girl.

WHAT IS THE HARDEST SCIENCE PROJECT YOU'VE EVER WORKED ON? The hardest science project I worked on was my senior design project in college which involved creating an oxygen generation system. It involved a tremendous amount of calculus and experimentation. But in the end, it was worth it. My team members and I learned a lot, and we won the Senior Design Project Award for our class.

WHAT DID YOUR CLASSMATES THINK OF YOUR PASSION FOR SCIENCE? Actually, I never felt that my classmates thought anything unusual about my passion for science. I think it was a trait that was respected by my peers.

DO YOU THINK MORE GIRLS ARE GETTING INTO SCIENCE? I do believe more girls are getting into science as they realize how fascinating and always changing the field is.

HOW CAN SCHOOLS, TEACHERS, AND OTHER ADULTS ENCOURAGE YOUNG GIRLS TO DO MORE SCIENCE? It's important that students are introduced to science in the classroom at very early ages. Girls are as naturally inquisitive as boys, and if they are exposed to science at a young age, I'm sure they will embrace it. Teachers and other adults can serve as wonderful role models and encourage girls to become actively involved in STEM activities. They can speak to girls about science, technology, engineering, and math and demonstrate the role science plays in everyday life.

WHAT ADVICE DO YOU HAVE FOR GIRLS? Believe in yourself and have confidence in your abilities. Always strive to do your very best, but recognize that you don't have to be perfect!

IF YOU HAD YOUR DREAM JOB, WHAT WOULD IT BE? At this point in my career, my dream job would be convincing girls all over the country to pursue careers in science and engineering; working with educational systems from elementary school through college to recognize the value of girls in STEM fields; and stimulating change.

WHAT ATTRACTED YOU TO SCIENCE? I loved chemistry, math and understanding how things worked.

WHAT INSPIRED YOU? My love of science and math.

HAVE YOU HAD ANY ROLE MODELS? Yes, I have had many role models. Role models are incredibly important through every phase of your career. There was only one senior woman chemist when I started working. It was difficult. Yet through the years, I have met many more women who have been great role models for me, particularly in encouraging me to believe in myself.

WHAT ADVICE DO YOU HAVE FOR GIRLS WHO WANT TO PURSUE A CAREER IN SCIENCE? Just do it! You will never regret it. It's fascinating and challenging, and you will be making the world a better place!

 **AND**

Know How®   Know How®

EXPLORING CAREERS
Make a Plan!
www.girlsknowhow.com

When I grow up, I would like to be a:

_____

_____

Describe why you would like this job. (For instance: I like to be active, I'm good at math or science, I like to read or write. I like adventure, travel, helping people, it pays a lot.)

1._____

2._____

Whom do I know with a job in this field?_____

Does anyone famous have this type of job? _____

What will I need to do this job well? (check all that apply)

____ Good grades

____ High school education

____ Some college or more school after high school

____ A special skill (what is it?)_____

____ Special training (what kind?)_____

____ Other_____

140

What attitudes/characteristics will help me succeed?

___ Honesty	___ Hardworking
___ Leadership	___ Creative
___ Teamwork	___ Other _____
___ Communicator	___ Other _____
___ Organized	___ Other_____

How can I learn more about this job?

___ Get a book from the library

___ Interview someone who has this job

___ Research this profession on the Internet
(with parents' permission)

___ Spend a day at work with someone who has this job

___ Look for the kinds of jobs in this field listed in career
search websites or newspaper employment sections

I PLEDGE TO LEARN MORE ABOUT
CAREER OPPORTUNITIES

List what you will do to learn more about this job:

1. This week, I will_____

2. This month, I will_____

3. Next month, I will_____

Signed_____ Date_____

Vocabulary Word Match

Match each word from the left column with the correct definition in the right column by drawing a line to connect them.

Word	Definition
A. acidic	1. Process of combining raw materials
B. alkaline	2. A branch of knowledge dealing with living organisms and vital processes
C. astronomy	3. The application of science and mathematics by which the properties of matter and the sources of energy in nature are made useful to people
D. biology	4. To force out or release
E. chemistry	5. Having properties of a soluble salt, a base
F. concoction	6. The study of objects and matter outside Earth's atmosphere
G. engineering	7. Having the reactions or characteristics of an acid
H. erupt	8. Science of composition, structure, and properties of substances and their transformations

Answers: A/7, B/5, C/6, D2, E/8, F/1, G/3, H/4

Vocabulary Word Match

Match each word from the left column with the correct definition in the right column by drawing a line to connect them.

Word	Definition
I. galaxy	9. Pitiful
J. genetics	10. Chart of the chemical elements
K. hypothesis	11. Serious, sedate
L. incredulous	12. An annual prize to encourage persons who work for the interests of humanity
M. nanorobot	13. A large group of stars and other matter
N. Nobel Prize	14. A science that deals with matter and energy and their interactions
O. pathetic	15. A tiny machine that performs a specific task with precision
P. periodic table	16. Amazed
Q. physics	17. The science of heredity and variation of organisms
R. solemn	18. A theory that explain a principle operating in nature

Answers: I/13, J/17, K/18, L/16, M/15, N/12, O/9, P/10, Q/14, R/11

143

Famous Women in Science Matching Game

Match each person from the left column with what
she is known for in the right column.

Person	**What She is Known For**
A. Barbara McClintock	1. World's foremost expert on chimpanzees and a conservationist
B. Elizabeth Blackwell	2. American astronomer who discovered a comet
C. Jane Goodall	3. The first woman in the US to receive a medical degree
	4. A pioneer in genetics who won a Nobel Prize
D. Mae Carol Jemison	5. A physicist and chemist who conducted research on radioactivity; Nobel Prize winner
E. Maria Mitchell	6. Chemical engineer, physician, and astronaut
F. Marie Curie	

Answers: A/4, B/3, C/1, D/6, E/2, F/5